Just A Number

L.M. Mountford

Edited by readabit: Copy Editing and Proofreading Services Est 2018
L.M. Mountford -- 1st Ed.
ISBN: 978-1-913945-92-3

About the Author

Sign up for VIP newsletter below to enjoy free books, new releases, discounts, ARC opportunities AND receive a FREE steamy read -
LMMountford.com

L.M. Mountford's goal in life is to be unique, a character who stands out from the crowd that you just can't help remembering with a bemused chuckle.

A born and bred country boy from the southwest of England, he knew from an early age that he wanted to write and spent most of his time writing story ideas or playing Star Wars on his PlayStation.

Not much has changed over the years, though his stories have grown decidedly dirtier, and he swapped the Star Wars for Call of Duty.

Dubbed the Lord of Lust in 2019 and a firm believer that nothing sells like sex and violence, he loves writing about hard and gritty romantic thrillers, loaded with action men, sassy heroines, and a whole lot of dirty, sexy heat.

Bibliography

**For a complete reading list, visit
LMMountford.com/bibliography/**

Collections
Deliciously Sinful Liaisons
Sweet Temptations Box Set
Romancing the Tropics
Just a Number
<u>Alpha Men of the Otherworld</u>
Rogue Warrior
<u>Rogue</u>
The Sweet Temptations Series
The Babysitter
The Boss's Daughter
Just Friends Series
Just Once
Broken Heart Series
Broken
Tropical Cocktail Romance
Tequila Sunset
Beneath the Sheets
Confessions of a Trophy Wife
Forbidden Desire
Stand-alone Titles
Uncovered
Serving the Senator
Reckless
Training Tracey

JUST A *Number*

THE LORD OF LUST
L.M. MOUNTFORD

Forbidden
Desire
THE LORD OF LUST
L.M. MOUNTFORD

Forbidden Desire

THE LORD OF LUST

L.M. MOUNTFORD

Prologue

    Watching her son drive down the road, Elizabeth Clarke sighed heavily.

    Today should have been one of the happiest days of her life. He'd done it. After five years - five long years of waiting, procrastination and disappointment, he'd finally done it. Victor, her sweet baby boy, was finally moving out and going to university.

    It hadn't been easy. He'd done abysmally in his GCSEs, barely scraping a passing grade, so he'd taken a break to work and save some money before going out and blowing it under the guise of travelling. He'd wanted to find himself, he'd told her, see the world. And he had, from what she could gather. He'd seen the world, one club at a time.

She doubted she'd ever know what he'd got up to out there, and she didn't want to. He hadn't written or called, just turned up on the doorstep, then a few days later enrolled in the city college for various courses. He'd worked hard, got his head down, studied, and finally, he had done it.

She should have been ecstatic, proud, and practically bouncing off the walls. What mother wouldn't be?

Yet all Elizabeth felt was a sense of abandonment. He was going, leaving her all alone with…

Him.

The thought sent a shiver down her spine that had nothing to do with the autumn breeze whispering through her long raven hair.

When the car turned around the street's bend, time seemed to hold its breath and Elizabeth wanted so badly to bend the laws of space and time around that moment, that last glimpse of her son, and stretch it on for an eternity. Then he was gone and who knew when she would see him again.

Of course, deep, deep down, she knew she was being silly. Oxford wasn't exactly Beirut. Victor was just a few hours' drive away. Close enough that he could come home for every Sunday roast.

And go back after.

That bitter pill drove her back indoors.

Desperate to keep busy, she set about doing the one job that had always proved as a source of comfort to her - cleaning. There was usually so much she needed to do, so many jobs that had to be done. A household of a young adult male was one that never stayed clean and required constant attention. Unfortunately, there was now a very vital part of that equation, which was no longer prevalent in her life. Without which it no longer felt like home. Without Victor, it was just another immaculate showroom, a haunted residence for a lingering spirit, the ghost of a neat and impeccable mother, and the base-camp of her travelling salesman husband.

Elizabeth furrowed her brow with disgust as she looked upon the neat pile of stacked plates and dishes in her cupboard, laundry ironed and folded away, and practically sparkling worktops. Then she felt her stomach tighten.

How could it be? Was there something she had forgotten, no that couldn't be it. She had followed the same routine she had always done and yet, somehow; she had finished five hours' worth of work in less than half an hour.

With a dispirited sigh, she walked across her now impeccably clean kitchen and fell into one of her dining table chairs. Resting her head in her hands, she tried to think of something, anything, to do.

God, how had her life come to this?

Patrick, he was why. That bastard had always been the source of her misery.

In school she'd always been outgoing, adventurous, the popular girl, always doing something. Be it tennis training or dance classes, going out with friends or babysitting the neighbourhood's kids - anything that would get her out of the house.

Then Patrick had entered her life and less than five months after her eighteenth birthday, they were married.

He'd been so handsome then. They'd made a lovely photo couple. The strapping rugby captain, all muscle and easy smiles, with the leggy athletic beauty on his arm in flowing white lace. The gown had been a work of art. It took a lot of looking in the photos to see the bump, the memento of a night she could only remember as an alcoholic haze, but that would completely reshape her life.

It had been a small ceremony for family and friends. Then he'd promptly whisked her across to the small house his parents had bought them on the over-side of the county, near where Somerset met Devonshire in one of the areas of many sleepy little villages. Ideally located for Victor's new role in the family business, but far away from her friends and family.

So, she'd become a mother and a housewife. The iconic role reversal from party girl and athlete to domestic goddess. And she'd revelled in it, the challenge of being a new mother, the thrill of bringing life into the world.

For Patrick, however, the switch had come as a nasty shock.

The walking, talking definition of a good time Charlie, his family had set him up in a role he'd been born to, salesman for their peat factory. And if the idea of going from garden centre to garden centre, sweet talking them into buying his family's products, hadn't quite lived up to the fast-talking rugby star's dreams of adult life, then he certainly hadn't bargained on all his hard work going to support his wife and child.

Or that he'd have to keep it in his pants.

She gave a dry laugh at the notion, before her eyes suddenly lit up.

Jennifer!

Chapter One

Years ago, the road had been a quiet snaking stretch of tarmac, but back in 1993, work had begun on a site that would become one of the UK's largest shopping outlet villages. In less than a year, Clarke's Village had transformed the A-39 into a bustling thoroughfare that during rush hour could be lined with bumper-to-bumper congestion. At ten in the morning, however, when all the rest of the world was being swept up in the ebb and flow of everyday life, there was very little in the way of traffic.

Sleek and polished to a high shine, the electric blue Audi TT convertible sped along the snaking stretch of single-lane tarmac. Heedless of the rain pelting the windscreen, Elizabeth kept her foot to the floor, relishing in the sweet rush of adrenaline as she sped through the numerous villages dotting the A-39.

She loved driving.

Fast driving was like great sex. It was freedom, a complete surrender to the moment. Behind the wheel, she forgot the disappointments, forgot the broken dreams, her sham of a marriage. She forgot all the downward slopes her life had taken. There was only the road, the rush, and the sexy throb of the engine purring through her. It was her escape.

There was no warning for the turning, just a sudden gaping maw in the surrounding woodland as the tarmac branched off. Used to the turn, Elizabeth dropped a gear and dragged the wheel around, adding just a dab of brake as the TT swung gracefully round the hairpin, then corrected for the straight and sped on. It was a reckless manoeuvre, stupid even in the rain along such a treacherous blind turn, but the momentary, stomach flipping rush made the risks seem rather insignificant.

Of course, she never had much to worry about in her Audi. The TT responded to her every command like the fine German engineered automobile it was.

Which was good, because off of the A-39, the way became a snaking lane of old tarmac and blind turns behind any number of which could await the hulk of an oncoming tractor or bus.

She floored it, and the Audi turned from a purring kitten to a raging tiger. It roared and kept roaring until she pulled into the familiar L-shaped driveway of *Forbidden Fruit* Cottage.

Despite its name, *Forbidden Fruit* Cottage was, in fact, a bungalow. A stately bungalow, though, with numerous extensions and surrounded by three acres of private land. It also happened to be the only property within two miles.

Heedless of the rain, Elizabeth got out of the sports car and sauntered up to the front door. Overhead, the sky was dark and subdued; the sun blotted out by the canopy of thick grey clouds. The rain, that had been a mere trickle when she set off, fell in a continuous sheet that drenched her from head to toe in the few strides to the front step.

All too aware of the icy rivulets running down the back of her neck, she raised a hand to knock, only for the door of heavy English oak, painted a deep blue with a plaque stamped *Forbidden Fruit*, to suddenly swing inward.

Elizabeth felt her breath catch.

Oh my…

Chapter Two

"Well, this is certainly a pleasant surprise. Hello there, Mrs Clarke." Hugh Becket could barely keep his grin at bay as he opened the door. *Damn, she's still so fucking gorgeous.*

"Oh…" Elizabeth had the deer in headlights look as she took him in. "Ugh, hi Hugh, is your mum in?"

"I'm afraid you just missed her. She and the old man have flown south for the winter and left me here to mind the fort." As he spoke, he eyed her hungrily, giving her a slow once over, then another for good measure. "You look good."

She always had.

"Thanks… err, you mind letting me in? It's pissing it down out here. I'm getting soaked."

Good to know.

"Sure, I'll get you a towel." He stepped aside to let her pass, his eyes dropping down to admire her backside as she passed. It took a feat of Herculean endurance for him not to whistle. Drenched as they were, her already skinny jeans moulded to her deliciously curved backside like a second skin. And that spaghetti top didn't exactly leave much to the imagination, either.

Suddenly very aware of the erection straining against the front of his own jeans, he pulled the door shut and wheeled around to the airing cupboard. There, he busied himself with rummaging through the ample assortment of towels on the shelves, careful to take just long enough for the very prominent bulge to diminish, for the most part, anyway. However, the task was made all the more difficult by the fact he could practically feel her eyes now travelling over him.

It was only when he was certain she would grow suspicious by his prolonged search that he reluctantly turned back and handed her a fluffy pink towel. At the time, though, her eyes were already a little further south, and they seemed to grow two sizes too big when they fixed on his groin. Which, in turn, responded to the attention.

Oh… shit.

"Can I get you anything? Tea? Coffee?" Hugh quickly asked, careful to keep his voice level even as she openly ogled him for a moment before dragging her eyes away.

"Err, tea, please. I could murder a brew." With that, she snatched the towel and fled into the living room.

Oh God, was that monster his cock or did he just stick a bloody cucumber down his trousers?

Furiously scrubbing her hair with the towel, Elizabeth felt her cheeks burning at the memory of the appendage straining against Hugh's trousers.

Oh fuck, he's huge… Did I do that to him?

The thought came out of nowhere and sent a pulse of heat straight down to her clit. Shocked, she immediately tried to brush it aside, but then couldn't help remembering the way he'd been watching her, the hot predatory gleam in his eyes as he'd looked her over.

She knew that look. It was a hot look, dark and hungry and very, very dangerous in the eyes of a young stud.

She'd seen it a lot when she was younger. On Saturday nights out when she went out to hit the town with her girlfriends. The clubs and bars would be thronged with packs of men who'd watched them with that same look. Like packs of wild dogs, eyeing up a fresh juicy bit of meat. Some of Patrick's mates had given her that same look over the years too, when they'd had a few too many and were likely to get handsy…

But to see Hugh giving her that same look. No, it couldn't be.

She'd known him and his mother for years, since he and Victor were kids in playschool. He was young enough to be her son. He was her friend's son, and her own son's best friend. And she was too old for him, much too old.

I'm old enough to be his mother.

"Tea's up!"

Her heart leapt at the husky voice.

Aimlessly scrubbing her hair, she swung around to find Hugh standing in the doorway, holding two steaming mugs. The vision was as breath-taking as it had been when he had been standing in the doorway. The image of him, in those casual *distressed* jeans and tight shirt, radiating such raw masculinity, an alpha male at ease in his territory, made her long to be twenty years younger.

He placed them on the coffee table.

"Still lots of milk and three sugars, right?"

Placing the towel over the headrest of one of the two matching armchairs that encircled one side of the table, she sat in one corner of the sofa that sat opposite. Able to practically feel the heat of his eyes on her skin through her clothes, she picked up the mug and sipped. Sweet and just that little bit shy of hot. Perfect.

"Cheers."

Elizabeth sipped and sipped until she knew she couldn't avoid talking to Hugh any longer without seeming rude. Then she mentally kicked herself. She was being ridiculous.

This was Hugh, just Hugh. It didn't matter that he had grown into a smouldering and sexy-as-hell Adonis. It was still Hugh. She focused on that, trying to think of the little boy she'd used to watch play in the park.

"So, Jen and Mike took off to the sun and gave you run of the house, huh? Where'd they go?"

"Gran Canaria," he answered, sitting beside her. As it was a two-seater, there was just enough room on the sofa for them both, just. "Dad scored a big commission, so they rented a condo out there for the month to celebrate."

"Lucky for some…" Elizabeth could feel herself shaking from his closeness. His tone was offhand and casual, but the way the smokiness of his voice curled around the words, he might as well have been whispering dirty fuck-me-talk right in her ear. "So, does this mean you've finished your pupillage?"

He picked his own mug up off the glass tabletop. "Yep, I'm now a fully certified and experienced lawyer."

"That's great." Her breath caught as he drank, her eyes immediately fixing on the subtle movements of his throat as he swallowed. Then she noticed his eyes, those intense, baleful blue eyes, burning bright against the inky dark of his pupils, watching her over the rim. She quickly looked away. "What are you going to do now? Take a break here while your parents are away, then head off back to the city? Get snapped up by some big firm and become a hotshot city lawyer? I could just see you in the Old Bailey, parading around in your robe and wig. Then hitting the streets with your expensive tailored suits and flash super car to turn all the girls heads. You were always a flash git, even when you and Victor were kids."

"Ouch," he mocked a hurt look. Then, putting the mug down, he rounded on her, the force of his presence enough to have her edging back into the sofa. "No, actually I'm here to stay. I took a job with a small firm down in Taunton. And I'm not involved in criminal law. I handle insurance."

"Insurance?"

"Yeah, insurance, and a bit of property law. It's less glamorous but steadier." As he spoke, Elizabeth couldn't help noticing he was edging closer. "And my clients aren't likely to throw acid in my face if I can't get them off."

Their growing proximity had awareness tingling through her arms, and heat gathering in the pit of her belly. "Fair point. So, you've just moved back into your old room? Aren't you a bit… err, *big* for that now?"

"A little." He teased and actually winked at her. "That's why I'm kipping in the spare room while I look for a place of my own."

"To rent?"

"Afraid so."

He was getting closer, too close.

"Well, it shouldn't take long to find somewhere, if you know where to look. You know, there are some delightful places over my way." Fuck, why had she said that?

"I remember." His voice lowered, growing hotter like the space between them. "You'll have to show me around. Give me the grand tour."

In spite of herself, Elizabeth's heart leapt at the idea.

"Sure, pop round anytime you're free and I'd be happy to show you the neighbourhood." God, what was she saying? She really needed to stop talking now. But she couldn't stop herself. It had just come out as her mind swam with the thought of him and her, alone, that body pushing up against her, all hard and male, his wicked mouth doing unspeakable things.

No, this wasn't good. She needed to get things onto a safer ground. "I know Victor would love it. You haven't seen him in ages. And it's such a great place to start a family. I'm sure your girlfriend will love it."

He smirked, as if he could see how close she was to snapping. And revelled in it. "Well, that sounds great. All I need to do now is to find a wife."

"Oh, so there's no one…"

"Oh, there's someone," he said. "There has been for a long time. She just doesn't know it *yet*."

Elizabeth felt a lump developing in her throat, her heart racing like a bird in a cage. "Well, I'm sure she's a very special girl."

"She is, but I'm not really interested in girls." He closed the gap, his big hand moving to gently rest on her denim encased thigh. "I prefer more mature women. Women who know what they want and how to get it."

She wanted him.

Wanted to touch him, taste him, bite him.

Wanted to lick her way down those delicious abs, tear those damn jeans off with her teeth, and suck his big fucking cock until-

He kissed her hungrily, all heat and instinct.

Chapter *Three*

She gasped, a soft whimper of protest, as the feeling of his lips crushing against hers set every nerve in her alive, but she didn't pull away. She didn't resist as his tongue danced across the roof of her mouth, ravishing her with lush licks that made her toes curl before entangling with hers. Nor did she try to escape when his powerful hands enveloped her, cupping her buttocks with exquisite force and dragging her across, so his resurrected cock pushed against the throbbing heat at her centre.

Then she was straddling his lap, the softness of his hair tickling the skin between her fingers as she fisted it and kissed him back, and nothing seemed to matter.

She didn't know what she was doing, but suddenly she didn't care.

She didn't care that it was wrong. Didn't care that he was her son's best friend. Didn't care that he was half her age.

She didn't care that she was a married woman.

He was just too much, too much for her to resist, to deny.

Hugh groaned, a low throaty sound when she sucked his tongue, the throbbing purr tingling down her spine to spike in her clit as his fingers squeezed her bum, crushing her to him. The sting and his roughness turned her on all the more. Fuck, she'd forgotten how good this could feel.

How good it should feel.

It had been so long since a man had made her feel like this, she couldn't help her little squeak of protest when he pulled away. Even so, a part of her screamed that it was for the best. They couldn't do this. It was wrong; it was so very bad…

"Hugh!" His name left her in a hot breathy moan as his lips covered that sensitive spot behind her ear and sucked.

She couldn't believe what was happening. What she was doing.

It was so surreal, like she was waking from a dream but not quite all the way, and was now trapped in that void where dreams met reality.

She didn't do this. She'd never done anything like this.

But she'd wanted to. Fantasised about it. Dreamt about it, but never…

Heat, want, and greed surged through her as tingling sensations zapped through her from her head to the tips of her fingers and toes. Moans poured from her, hot and wanton. Somewhere in the back of her subconscious, she just registered the weight of his desire pushing against the heat throbbing in the cradle of her hips. The idea that she was affecting this young stud as potently as he was her was so exciting, she couldn't resist. She needed to touch him, feel him.

Her hands moved slowly, cautiously, almost ridiculously so, given their predicament. However, she couldn't help it. Half afraid the lightest touch, too bold, might shatter the spell and repulse him.

So, Elizabeth clung to him, her body crushed to his, hands pawing at his back through his shirt. He felt so hard. Not bulky the way bodybuilders strived for, but solid, corded and toned. A slab of marble, chiselled layer by layer into a work of art, like Michael Angelo's *David* given life.

At any other moment, she might have wondered how the devil he had managed it, while at the same time juggling the hectic life of a lawyer in training. However, now, all she wanted was to see him, feel his skin, and worship him. If only his bloody shirt wasn't tucked so neatly into his jeans, barring her from immediate access. It just wasn't fair. It would take too long for her to pull it loose, and the act itself presented the considerable problem of having to take her hands off him.

Worse still, Hugh was faster and bolder, much bolder.

While his mouth worked her into a frenzy, ravishing her sensible tendons with licks and nips, one of his hands worked its way up beneath her top. It was cold against her heated skin, but the chill only added to the sensuousness of his touch. His fingers brushed over her naked flesh, up her midriff, over her ribs, gathering up the hem of her top as it went. He was careful to avoid her breasts, however, and neglect made her nipples ache as he pushed the garment up and over her bountiful cleavage.

He left the spaghetti-string top there, bunched and rolled up under her arms. With a final nip of her earlobe, he pulled back to admire his handiwork. In a dark, far-flung corner of her mind that was still capable of rational thought, a voice urged her to come to her senses and slap that smug look off his gorgeous face and cover herself.

She quickly pushed aside, however, when she saw the look in his eyes as he took her in. How long had it been since Patrick had looked at her like that? Had he ever?

He rumbled an approving purr. Deep and low, it thrummed through his body into hers wherever their skin touched, making her sex clench. Clearly, he liked what he saw, and the thought made her glad she'd worn the red lace bra adorned with black filigree.

It was a tad too expensive and ornate to be considered practical, but the way it pushed her tits up and lifted the years, made the expense a thing of little account.

Her ass also happened to look great in the matching thong, if she said so herself.

"Mmm… your tits are amazing."

His words thrummed through her, straight down to her pulsing clit, as the pad of his thumb brushed brazenly over her breasts, teasing around her bra. Just inches from where she needed it.

"You know, I used to dream about fucking them when I was younger. I'd jerk off thinking about burying my cock in them while that mouth sucked me off, but what really made me blow was thinking about them bouncing while I fucked you. Especially when I went balls deep, and you begged me to give it to you, to take your creamy cunt..."

Her breath came in short gasps that were only slightly due to the way he was plumping her cleavage, that huge palm rubbing over her nipple through the lace in the most exquisite torture. His dirty words were a seduction in their own right. The thought of him stroking that monster while he dreamed of having his way with her. It was more than she could stand.

No man had ever treated her like this. He was rough and knew what he wanted, knew what she wanted, even if she didn't know it. He made her feel. Made her lose herself in the moment. She couldn't think. She couldn't remember why she was there, or where she was, or even what had brought her to this sofa with this stranger.

This wasn't the boy she'd known.

That boy had grown up. Become a man. A man who took what he wanted.

And he wanted her.

Wanted her so lustily, he ripped the bra away like it was dental floss. With a flick of his wrist, he discarded the expensive piece of lingerie, banished it to a place out of sight. Then the damp, delicious heat of his mouth replaced it, sucking in her nipple, making her gasp ragged breaths.

"Oh god, what… what are you doing to me…" she panted, her back arching as he brought his other hand up to cup and knead her neglected tit. Sparks and starbursts sizzled through her as he worshipped her breasts. Then abruptly, he switched, and his fingers rolled her slick right bud into a heightened state of arousal while his tongue swirled around and around her left in ever shrinking circles, until she just wanted to scream.

Somehow, Hugh knew just how to play her body like a fiddle.

Grabbing and squeezing, biting and sucking, rolling and pinching her nipples, he made her feel things…

He made her feel like a woman again. Made her feel all the things she'd forgotten in her years of captivity. Her years of bondage, in matrimony, bound to a weak, whimpering sham of a man.

Made her feel that feeling again. That slick heat throbbing so insistently down in her centre and the delicious friction that accompanied it every time she moved.

He made her feel things, and she wanted more.

"Mmm… Yeah… that's it… fuck… you bad boy!"

The words were out before she really knew what she was saying. Almost by their own volition, her hands had threaded through his hair, both pulling him to her and steadying her as she ground her body into his.

And suddenly Elizabeth's entire world was focusing on that feeling of him sliding along her folds, through all the layers of lace and denim, to grind against her clit.

God! He feels even bigger than he looks…

The feeling brought the universe crashing down around her.

This wasn't right.

She couldn't do this.

She didn't do… this.

She was a respectable woman, a married woman. She didn't have random quickies with men half her age. She didn't shag strange men, even if they were the embodiment of a fucking sex god!

No! She couldn't do this… she mustn't … she … she … No … No…

"No!"

In other circumstances, the look of stunned disbelief on Hugh's face as he jumped back would have looked rather comical. However, Elizabeth was in too much of a rush to appreciate it.

"I'm… sorry… that… that was a mistake. I should… I shouldn't have done that." Scrambling back off of the sofa and to her feet, she pushed her top down, being careful to walk around the coffee table and put as much space between her and her ravisher as possible as she did.

Then, without waiting for his reply, she was out of the room, down the hall, through the door, in her car and gone.

Chapter *Four*

Back home, in the safety of her kitchen, Elizabeth could barely keep her hands from shaking as she sipped her tea. The residual arousal clawed at her, thrumming her nerves like taut guitar strings.

The tea took the edge off a little.

"God! What was that?"

She couldn't believe what she'd done, and with Hugh, of all people.

It was like something out of a bloody porno. Throwing herself at a hot stud after seeing he had a gigantic cock. All that was missing was the delivery man with a funny accent and the big sausage pizza.

Oddly, though, she didn't feel the least bit guilty. Frustrated, sure. Disappointed, maybe. Horny, fuck yeah! But no guilt.

Why would she? Patrick had his indiscretions, his little playthings, his… *whores!*

So what if she had a little slip with a dark and dashing toy-boy? She was a woman. She had needs.

But to do it, or nearly do it, with Hugh!

Her friend's son. Hell, he was her own son's friend, and not just any friend, his best friend. He was as off limits as it got. And all the hotter for it.

She quickly chugged her drink, desperate to quell the memory of his hands on her, the searing heat of his touch sizzling across her skin, working its way too – *No!*

Damn it all to hell, she needed to get laid. That would get it all out of her system. How long had it been anyway? Two months, maybe even three? Yes, that was it. She needed to get fucked, that was all. She needed…

She paused, an idea lurching to mind, and she looked to the kitchen window. The sky overhead was still grey and overcast, growing darker by the second as dusk crept in, but the rain was stopping.

Her lips broke into a sly smile when her gaze landed on the large and luxurious hot tub on the back porch.

Keeping his foot down hard on the accelerator, Hugh turned off the Bridgwater Road and sped down the residential street towards the Clarke family's household on the outskirts of the Bampton area. A glance at his Omega told him it was a little after eight. *Not much further now…*

He didn't know what he was going to say, but he just couldn't leave things standing with Elizabeth the way they were. It felt like he'd been waiting his whole life to have a chance with Elizabeth Clarke, and now that he'd tasted her, he wasn't about to let her get away.

Not now, not after he'd waited for so long.

Heedless of the rain pounding his windscreen, he sped his BMW M5 down the residential streets, taking the swerving bends lined by detached red brick and grey stone homes like turns on the Nürburgring.

The years of going to and from Mrs Clarke's house with his mum had drilled the route into his memory, but it had been a while. He almost thought he'd gone too far until he spotted Elizabeth's Audi and pulled in behind it on the drive.

Most of the ground floor lights in the house were on, but, much to his delight, there was no sign of Mr Clarke's Alfa Romeo 4C. The old git might have complicated things, but if he was away on one of his infamous *business* trips, then his wife would be all alone.

And if her performance in his parent's living room was any indication, she desperately needed a little TLC. Well, maybe a little less T and a whole lot of L.

Shutting the quietly purring BMW down, he slid out of the driver's seat, pocketed the fob, and walked up the drive to the front door. His mouth suddenly drier than the desert, he tapped his knuckles against the painted timbers of the front door.

Against the soft patter of the rain, the knocks echoed like the blasts of a cannon. Suddenly nervous, Hugh couldn't help brushing himself down, trying to smooth his clothes as he awaited an answer.

None came.

He knocked again, a little harder this time. Still no answer.

Okay, time for Plan B.

There was a time when he and Victor knew all the secret ways in and out of each other's homes. Now the memories came swimming back. Dropping down into a crouch, he slinked round the edge of the building, beneath the overhanging ledge of the family room's window seat, and through the flower beds. The fake rock was exactly where he remembered, nestled into the roots of a stump that had once been a towering apple tree.

Retrieving the key, he rose up and moved around to the side of the house and unlocked the padlock securing the ornate iron side gate between the house and the garage.

A quick open-palmed push had the gate swinging open with a low creak that practically screamed his presence to the world. Someone obviously hadn't been keeping on top of the building maintenance.

The alleyway between the two buildings leading to the back garden was inky black all the way to the steps of the back porch, but he could hear commotion up ahead. A sound like water bubbling on the hob.

There was something else too, something softer, almost indistinguishable from the background, but that made his dick instinctively stir to life. He couldn't believe his luck. Heart hammering excitedly in his chest, he followed the sounds and, edging forward, slowly peered around the edge.

Elizabeth was in her hot tub, her head propped on a rolled towel beside an almost empty wine glass. It was a very deep model, more than half sunken into the porch, yet the steaming, bubbling water came all the way up to her shoulders. Nonetheless, the tops of her breasts were clearly visible as, eyes closed and biting her lip, she arched her back; her left hand fondling her cleavage.

In the soft golden hue of the back-porch light, it was obvious she had forgone a swimsuit.

Hugh greedily drank in the view. He'd been dreaming of this moment, picturing it ever since he first started noticing girls, no, since he'd started to notice women. He'd never been really interested in girls. They were always so prissy and uptight, or always playing games. They didn't know what they wanted or how to satisfy a man. And while their bodies were fun to play with, they could never compare to the lush, full curves of a mature woman.

Mrs Clarke was the very epitome of a mature, beautiful woman.

His fantasy.

His goddess.

Patrick, that son of a bitch, didn't deserve her. He'd neglected and abandoned her, so tonight, Hugh would make her his.

He could just hear her panting, soft, wanton moans. They were music to his ears and almost without realising what he was doing, his free hand began fumbling with the button of his far too tight trousers. He could scarcely breathe from the tightness. He had to be set free, to relieve the tension building in his groin…

"Mmm…" she purred, hot and breathy. "Fuck… Yes… give me that cock… oh-my-god… I need it, yes…"

Nearly tearing his trousers open, he grabbed his cock. He couldn't see her other hand, but he didn't need to. He could picture her fingering her slick wet pussy, working herself up, first one, then two fingers, her hips rolling and growing more urgent as she got closer. He matched her pace, pumping his cock, the shaft slick with precum, and greedily devoured the sight of her playing with her dusky pink nipple. Twisting and tugging, imitating the very treatment he'd given it just hours earlier.

He answered her low moans by thrusting himself into the tight coil of his fist. Still pent up from their earlier encounter, Hugh knew he wouldn't last long, and though he'd seen his share of pornography, this was the first time he'd ever watched a woman masturbate in real life. It was the most erotic thing he'd ever seen.

Porn was cheap titillation. Sex manufactured with all the passion and intensity stripped away, like Ikea flat pack furniture.

Once you'd seen one, you'd seen them all.

This was anything but cheap titillation. This was seduction. Hugh would never tire of watching her.

She was a living woman, repressed and denied, A font of pent up sexual tension just starting to bubble to the surface and in desperate need of a good, hard-

"Oh, God... that's it baby... pound that pussy... oh god... I'm gonna- fuck, I'm cumming, I'm cumming... Hugh!"

Oh shit!

He froze, his fist tight just under the head. The sound of her calling out his name in that ragged breathy voice, triggered a chain reaction that pushed him over the edge.

He came hard, shooting a thick stream of cum that arced into the darkness. Yet his eyes never strayed from the view of Elizabeth as her own climax ripped through her.

The orgasm she'd reached while thinking of him...

Chapter Five

Elizabeth had never expected to be doing this. She'd only wanted a soak in the hot tub, but then everything had spiralled out of control.

Her idea had worked.

As she lay soaking in the hot water, all her tension had just seemed to melt away and she was content to do nothing more than let the jets work their magic, carrying her away, back to that sofa in Jennifer's living room.

Hugh was with her, above her, topless, with his jeans hanging low on his hips.

He was kissing her again, hot and hungry kisses. She could feel his desire for her burning strong and pressing demandingly between her thighs as he rolled his hips.

Sinking deeper into her fantasy, heat that had nothing to do with the hot tub spiralled around her belly.

A long sigh passed her lips as her hands mirrored her fantasy. Already stiff, her nipples tingled as her fingers teased around them and sensation rippled down her spine in a rush that had her cupping and squeezing her heavy bosom while her other palm moved down her belly.

"Mmm… Oh yes, you're such a bad boy…"

Hugh laid her down across the sofa, his hands ripping the clothes from their bodies. Then he was covering her, and she could barely keep from drooling as he took himself in hand, stroking from base to tip so that a milky drop appeared.

She wanted to lick it, taste it. No, taste him, and more. So much more. Only he was faster…

She moaned, biting her lip in pleasure as the feeling of a finger sliding through her sent a white-hot shiver of delight coursing through her centre. It was a poor substitute for a real cock, but she'd missed the feeling of having something inside her for so long that she hardly cared and began rocking against the invading digit.

"Fuck… Yes… give me that cock… oh-my-god… I need it, yes…"

Oh god, what was wrong with her?

It had never been like this, even in those years after Victor was born and Patrick had spent more and more time away on business trips. She had kept her composure and forewent the sexual urges. Life had been simpler back then. Her days had been full, the nights lonely, but she had been too preoccupied with her role of being a young mother to give much thought to her neglected libido.

Now, however, things were different. Victor was away at university. She was alone, and what she had once thought insignificant was resurfacing with a vengeance.

She was shaking, every nerve in her body tingling with sensations as she used her thumb to play with her clit while working two fingers in and out. Almost mindless with the clawing need to cum, her body tensed under the duress of hot waves and she moaned again, only louder, not caring who heard as she came for the first time in longer than she could remember.

God, how had she gone without a man for so long?

Then, as the waves receded and afterglow settled, she felt it.

It was only a momentary distraction. A prickling sensation of awareness that tickled the back of her neck and tingled through her skin, but it was enough.

Someone was watching her.

The thought had her on instant alert, the vulnerability of her position, and the repercussions of what she had been doing, suddenly glaringly oblivious. Nervously, she looked up and around at the upper windows of the homes that encircled her back garden. They were all dark behind the drawn curtains and blinds, however, that did not distract her from the certainty that someone was out there.

She could feel their eyes on her and strangely, rather than feeling violated by the intrusion, it was turning her on all over again. The idea that someone she couldn't see was watching her through the gloom thrilled her, made her belly flutter and core pulse excitedly. It was such an exciting feeling, it almost tempted her to give her audience an encore.

God, when had she become such an exhibitionist?

From his hideaway, Hugh had a near perfect view of Elizabeth rising up out of the hot tub and towelling herself dry. She seemed to take her time and spent much more time than necessary patting away every lingering drop of water before wrapping the towel around herself and hurrying back into the house.

All right, genius, what now?

Tucking his still-stiff erection back into his trousers, he glanced back down the pathway. He could go back the way he'd come and try the front door again. She would hear him this time and answer, but then what would he say? He hadn't given the matter any thought on the drive over, and after what he'd just witnessed, he'd probably be as tongue tied as a virgin on a date with Madison Ivy.

Or he could go home, think on the matter a little bit, then come back in the morning, after she'd…

After she'd what? Calmed down? He dismissed the notion immediately. He wouldn't go back, not now. He'd waited too long for this chance. He couldn't, he wouldn't, he…

He wheeled around, crossed the garden, and stormed up the porch to the back door. Knowing it was unlocked, he twisted the knob and pushed the door open.

Elizabeth stood with her back to him, her towel replaced by a black silk dressing gown that barely covered her lush derriere. He could hear her humming a low melody as she busied herself with fastening the belt around her waist. Unable to resist the opportunity, he crossed the kitchen in quick strides and reached out a hand to cup her arse.

Totally oblivious to his presence, Elizabeth shrieked and whirled around, her eyes widening at the sight of him.

"Hugh! What are you-"

Her reprimand quickly died as he seized her lips with his, silencing her with a deep kiss. For one harrowing moment, she tried to break free, wriggling and squirming and pushing against the solid mass enveloping her. However, his powerful hands held her close, crushing her to him. Then his tongue swept past her lips, and the fight left her completely. He felt her relax, and he urged her back, his big hands squeezing her butt, then hoisting her up onto the counter.

There were no words or gestures. No explanations given or required.

His need for her was like an all-consuming fire in his blood, a raging inferno that would not be sated until he had devoured every bit of her. With a mind to do just that, he took advantage of his new leverage to deepen the kiss, their tongues becoming locked in an intimate dance that had them both panting with passion as he moved in between her splayed thighs.

She braced her hands against his torso, urgently pushing his jacket down his arms before moving up to bury themselves in his hair. Their hips were rolling together in synchronised motions and they wantonly devoured one another until the need for oxygen forced Elizabeth to pull away. However, Hugh was not so easily deterred and trailed kisses along her jaw before bending down to nip along her neck, making her gasp and moan in undisguised delight. "Oh God … No … We can't … we shou-oh!"

Her protestations were weak and lacked any conviction when spoken amidst such needy tones. Paying them no heed, he crouched down between her thighs and hitched her long legs over his shoulders. She didn't fight him, and he turned his eyes up to hold her gaze as he dipped his head.

Elizabeth couldn't believe what was happening.

Everything was going so fast. One minute she was just wondering what she should do for dinner. The next she was being hoisted atop her kitchen cabinets, watching Hugh's gorgeous, chiselled face going down between her legs.

It was a scene taken straight out of her fantasies and when his tongue flicked over her still oversensitive clit, she completely forgot all of her earlier objections. Arching with a low moan, she shoved a hand into his hair, pulling his mouth against her. Her suddenly overheated sex rippled as his tongue plunged in and began feasting on her with deep, swirling licks.

"Mmm… you're so tasty Mrs Clarke…" Hugh growled, his tongue never ceasing in its exploration as he ate her hungrily. "I could eat your cunt all night."

He buried his face in her tender flesh, completely immersing him in her core as her cream flowed readily into his greedy mouth. She had a unique flavour, one he couldn't get enough of her, and sucked her folds before working his tongue in and out, orally fucking her into delirium.

"Hugh… Oh fuck!" Elizabeth was on the verge of losing all control. Her whole body was aquiver from the things his mouth was doing to her. Still sensitive from her self-induced climax, she knew it wouldn't be long before she reached her peak. Her thighs tightened instinctively, trying to hold him in place while she greedily bucked and ground her pelvis against him in a desperate attempt to make his tongue go as deep as possible.

This was something Patrick had never done for her. Though he expected it often, her loving husband never felt the need to return the favour. Hugh, however, was more than happy to attend to her, and oh God was he was so good at it. Already she could feel herself returning to the edge of that sweet precipice. Her hand clutched desperately at clumps of his hair as his tongue mercilessly pillaged her core, stretching to its limit and caressing her deeper than she'd ever thought possible. It felt like he was licking her everywhere at once.

Eager to give her what she craved, Hugh altered tactics and, with both arms coiled around her thighs, pivoted her up ever so slightly. This new position afforded him greater access to her body, and he didn't wait before switching to suckle her clit.

"Oh, sweet Jesus… Hugh, please, please… I… I… oh my god, you're going to make me cum again… yes, yes, yes, oh fuck I'm gonna cum, I'm gonna…"

She thought she was going to die.

When he sucked her little bundle of nerves, a thousand different explosions went off in her head at once. Oh yes, she was going to die. She was going to burn up in the fires of her own ecstasy.

"Yeah, cum for me, Mrs Clarke," Hugh growled, staring up at her, his gaze dark and hot with lust. "You're so fucking sexy. Feed me your wet cunt and cum on my face as I eat your pussy."

She looked so amazing like this, so dishevelled and uninhibited, so unlike the woman he had known while growing up.

Caught in his stare, Elizabeth couldn't look away. Even as the orgasm exploded through her, called up by his very command, she was possessed, rooted by the desire burning in his eyes, the sheer sensuality of watching him go down on her as waves rushed over her. They crested higher and higher until the storm passed, and it had reduced her to a panting mess.

Licking his lips clean, Hugh lowered her legs off of his shoulders and rose up to his full height between her drooping limbs. At some point, he must have unfastened his trousers. They were open and his cock stood rampant between muscular thighs, the wide crest poised at her cleft. With a roll of his hips, he dragged the weeping tip along her folds to nudge her oversensitive clit.

The contact sent a thrill through Elizabeth that made her back arch. She wanted this. No, she needed this, but not here, not in her kitchen.

"Take me to bed."

Chapter Six

Hugh Didn't question her decision. With a nod, he heaved her up and crushed her to him. Instinctively, she crossed her legs over his buttocks and swept her hands over his shoulders, scoring him lightly with her nails and marvelling at the wall of muscle beneath his shirt. He carried her effortlessly out of the kitchen, down the hall, and up the stairs to the master bedroom.

He didn't bother turning on the light. Elizabeth was glad of that. The darkness helped her nervousness, made her feel like she was somewhere other than her family home, and it hid the photos. They were many- and everywhere, photos of birthdays and events, of her family and friends, of Victor. She didn't think she could do this with him watching.

However, there was enough light for Hugh to discern the outline of the grand canopied king-size bed. He made straight for it, but he didn't notice the rug at its foot. He slipped, and they tumbled together onto the neatly made covers, with Elizabeth on top.

She felt a thrill shiver down her spine as she took in the sight of the young man lying beneath her, unable to keep the devious smirk from her lips.

Strong, intelligent, and handsome, there wasn't a red-blooded woman alive that wouldn't give her right arm just to have him look at them the way he was at her. And yet, at this moment, he only had eyes for her, the mother of his best friend. A middle-aged housewife who had given the best years of her life to a neglectful, drunkard and adulterer. What had she ever done to get so lucky?

Smirking wickedly, Elizabeth winked, then shuffled her butt back down his legs.

Hugh gave her a quizzical look. "Mrs Clarke?"

"I love it when you call me that," she purred, keeping her eyes locked on his until she found what she was looking for and gave a surprised gasp. "Wow, you've grown into such a *big boy*."

Then, with her eyes still burning into his, she dipped her head and dragged the flat of her tongue up the underside of his cock from root to tip before going to work on him.

Hugh groaned and fisted the sheets, unable to look away as she bowed her head. Those full pink lips stretched tight and gliding down his cock, sucking him in.

"Oh fuck, Mrs Clarke…"

Whenever he called her that, it just sounded so dirty. Elizabeth couldn't help moaning around her mouthful. And he was a mouthful. She'd wanted to take him all in, but he was much too big for that. Only a third of the way down and she was already at her limit. Yet that only made her feel naughtier. He just smelled so good, and his taste- she'd never known a man could taste so good. Pulling back, her cheeks hollowed as she sucked and mouthed his thick crown.

"Is this what you want, Hugh, your best friend's mum, sucking your cock?"

Releasing the head, she swirled her tongue around and around the wide crest, before pulling back to tease the tip with flicking licks. Then she was dragging the flat of her tongue up and down his length, like she was licking an ice lolly, and all the while still looking up into his eyes.

"Mmm… such a yummy cock. I bet you make all the girls choke with this big dick…"

It was too much. Hugh couldn't take it.

"Oh, shit!" he groaned, eyes rolling up and his head falling back into the bed's soft embrace.

Elizabeth grinned inwardly, relishing the feeling of his cock pulsing under her tongue. "I want it, you bad boy. Wanna feel this big dick splitting me open. I need it!"

Quick as a snake, Hugh lurched up, seized her around the waist and hurled her to the bed. Then, looming above her, he pulled his shirt over his head. With a flick of his wrist, he cast it aside. His shoes and trousers were gone just as quickly, leaving him standing before her in all his naked glory, the weak light glittering over his sculpted muscles and casting him in a godly radiance.

She didn't have time to enjoy the view, however. In the blink of an eye, he was on top of her. With a quick tug, he had her robe undone and over her head. She gasped at his sudden ferocity, his new dominance a complete turn on that had her all but panting as the weight of his erection settled against her throbbing clit.

"Ready?"

"Yes!" Elizabeth wanted to scream. What was he waiting for? Couldn't he see that she'd never been more ready for anything in all her life? "Yes, damn it, just fuck me, you bast-oh!"

Her back arched as her every sense was consumed by the delicious burn of his cock driving home. He filled her so completely, she could feel his every ridge and thick ropy vein coiled about his trunk. It was such a delicious sensation. She couldn't help fisting the sheets as her long legs closed around the sexy V-line of his waist and dug her heels into his flanks, urging him on.

Yet Hugh held firm. He had to.

Fuck, she felt so good, all hot, slick and so fucking snug. It was almost unbearable. It was only through force of sheer will that he was able to tear himself down from the edge before it was too late. Then her lush inner walls wrapped around him, squeezing his dick like a fist in a warm velvet glove. And it was too much.

He had to move.

"Oh god, oh shit… oh fuck!" Elizabeth felt ready to burst as Hugh started rolling his hips, drawing back, then driving home, going deliciously deep as the flair of his hips spread her legs back. His pace was intolerably slow, but with each fervent drive she could feel herself opening to him, her delicate tissues stretching around every delicious inch of him. It was so raw, so intense.

Sex with her husband was nothing compared to this. Even the way he was looking at her. Patrick had never looked at her that way. He didn't want to possess her, to own and use her as though she were property. He wanted simply to love her, to be with her in every way that two people could be. The way nobody had ever been with her before.

This wasn't just lust or longing, this was something more, something deeper, something both sacred and beautiful.

Elizabeth couldn't stand it. "Oh god, I'm cumming."

"That's it, cum for me, *Mrs Clarke*." His command was a low growl in her ear before he kissed her, smashing his mouth to hers, his tongue stroking hers as she came.

Shaking, riding the waves, Elizabeth clung to him, hands grabbing and clawing every bit of him she could reach, barely able to hang on. Desperate for more, she moved with him, grinding against each lunge of his big dick even as they sent her spiralling higher and higher.

Feeling her writhe under him, Hugh was certain he was orbiting madness.

It took all of his will not to give into his dark side, his primitive side. The debased animal that lurked in the heart of every man. The beast that yearned to take this woman, to make her beg and scream his name. It clawed at his resolve, whispering a sweet song of dominance and mastery. Yet he wanted this to be more than just fucking.

Now was his chance to show her, to prove to her, that there was more for her than just the mundane existence of a lonely housewife for her. That he was a better man than her good-for-nothing husband. His time had come and hooking an arm round her waist, he pulled her close, driving her hot little cunt all the way down to his root, as he reared back and pushed up onto his knees.

"Oh God!" Elizabeth gasped, ripping her lips from his in a long moan as his new angle of penetration scraped her sweet spot just right.

The way he held her had her hips pinned to his, and as he rocked back and forth, dragging her clit deliciously over his abdomen. The sensation was so intense it made her head spin. Completely absorbed in her own pleasure, her lips had formed an 'O' shape and with each jolting thrust, her whole body jumped delightedly to meet him, causing her enchantingly full breasts to bounce. "Yes, yes, yes! Harder baby! Please… fuck me harder!"

"Yeah, ride my dick Mrs Clarke, ride it!"

"Oh my god… so much… so deep… oh fuck… it's amazing!" She was shaking again, her whole body humming as waves of sensation washed through her and goose bumps rose up all over her skin.

"You love my cock, don't you?"

"Yes! I love it, fuck my pussy more, I want it, I love it"

"Is it better than your husband's?"

To emphasise his question, he buried himself in her warmth again and saw the dam inside her crack beneath a sudden mini climax that caused her eyes to roll. Her body trembled as liquid ecstasy rushed through her and Hugh watched with unabashed delight, fucking her through the pleasure with quick stabs of his cock.

"So … so much better, oh fuck. I had no idea what I've been missing… I… I never knew sex could be so… so good! Fuck me more! Make me take it! Use me like he never cou-oh!" The cry left her lips before her mind could register what she had said, yet it was too late. Her body was melting in a sea of liquid pleasure and all sense of words and thought had left her. Moaning hotly as she tossed her head from side to side, her sweat dampened mane of raven hair fanning out around her, she caught only the briefest glimpse of him smirking down at her. It was a very hot look on him. It made the throbbing knot in her centre pulse dangerously, pushing her towards her pleasure's violent pinnacle.

"And who is the best fuck of your life?" Perspiration glistened across his bronzed skin and a few salty drops rolled down his neck as he felt himself nearing his limit.

"You! Oh Fuck… you Hugh… it… oh god, yes… it was always you… so good… I can't take it… I'm… I'm cumming!"

Even as she spoke, she could feel her arms coiling around his neck as her arse gyrated in his lap. They were so close now, it perfumed her every gasping breath with his musky scent and she was suddenly aware of how hot his skin felt against her body. The sensations were so intense, her world had dissolved into a brilliant rush of colour and she couldn't tell where one tide of pleasure ceased and the next began as they merged into one continuous flood of glorious ecstasy.

Was she going mad?

Or perhaps this was what it felt like to die?

Maybe death by sex wasn't just some delightful male fantasy, and this terrific young stud had indeed fucked her into an early grave.

"Yeah, that's it, cum for me Mrs Clarke, cum all over my… my- oh fuck! I'm cumming too!"

The visual stimuli of her gorgeous naked body writhing and wriggling atop his pillaging shaft, combined with the feel of her juices coating him as her walls closed tight, sent him over the edge. After being restrained for so long, the force of his release was like nothing he had ever experienced, and a thunderous groan bellowed from his lips as his seed surged into her womb.

Still joined in the most intimate of fashions, they collapsed together in a tangled mass of limbs on the bed, their chests heaving with laboured breaths. Sweat made their bodies glisten in the low light, yet neither made any effort to move. Feeling safe and content in the others' presence, they fell into a blissful sleep.

Epilogue

Elizabeth didn't want to wake.

Usually, she was an early riser and would be up with the sun. There were chores to do, breakfasts to make, and an ever-mounting list of jobs. Her jobs.

However, today she just couldn't bring herself to do it. It felt safe here, safe and warm. Here she felt at peace, content.

Light, so dazzling with all the magnificence of the dawn, blanketed her naked body. Winter was coming. Its frosty breath wafted through the window, caressing her skin with soft and tantalising fingers fragrant with all the flavours of Autumn.

Half asleep, she trembled as the air teased down her back and arms, stirring goose flesh, and it was only when arms, strong as oak and corded with muscle, coiled around her waist, pulling her back against the wall of a hard male body lying beside *her that she settled. Satisfied to just lie back and enjoy the moment, Elizabeth made no effort to resist as he crushed her to him, a soft moan escaping her as her breasts were pressed into his chiselled torso and the weight of his cock rose up to nestle in the cradle of her thighs. It was such a delectable sensation, the feeling of his hands around her, his breath hot on her neck, the heat radiating off his body, enveloping her, dragging her back down into sweet serenity as she listed to the deep rhythmic drumming of his heart.*

And she couldn't remember ever feeling so sated.

Despite it all, she fought against the urge to curl into him, to sleep and prolong the moment across the boundless seas of eternity. Taken instead by the sudden need to see him, and an irrational fear that it might have all been a dream. A hot, wonderful, sweaty dream.

The greatest fucking dream of my life.

Just the memory of it stoked the embers in her core to new life. Suddenly more awake than asleep, she peeled her eyes back slowly to meet the stormy grey-blue eyes watching her from beneath sandy sleep-tousled hair.

"Mmm… good morning," he purred in that smoky voice that made her whole body tighten. Or maybe it was the way his mouth moved over the words, slow and seductive, pronouncing each syllable with delicious purpose. He had a very nice mouth. Thin peach coloured lips perfectly shaped with a sexy indent in the corner from where he had frequently bitten them when he was concentrating. A mouth made for kissing, licking, and doing the most wicked things. And that jaw, like an anvil with the perfect amount of rough to tease her inner thighs when he was tonguing her clit.

She couldn't help blushing at the memory, the heat in her core spreading out in a scarlet flush as she averted her gaze.

No one had ever looked at her the way he had just then. It was so intense, so intimate. Much too intimate. Like he was seeing her, truly seeing her. Seeing more than the neglected married woman in desperate need of a good shag. More than just Victor's mother. More than…

She couldn't bear it. "No."

"What?" he smirked, pulling her closer, practically skin to skin. He was hard, like chiselled stone, but they fit together perfectly. A carved marble Adonis shaped just for her.

"Don't look at me like that… it's embarrassing."

"I can't help it. Mmm… that blush is just so sexy." He dipped his head to nip the curve of her neck, his tongue quick to sooth the delicious hurt.

"No… please… you can't, I'm still sore- oh!" She gasped when he scraped that sweet spot behind her ear, her eyes rolling. His hand came up to knead her breast, thumb and forefinger, rolling her nipple so roughly she couldn't help arching into his palm.

"Mmm… you have amazing tits."

Tonguing the shell of her ear, Hugh seized upon Elizabeth's momentary distraction to push her back down onto the bed, caging her glorious naked body with his before taking a nipple into his mouth. He sucked greedily, and the delicious cocktail of heat and suction around her sensitive nub had her back arching, her fingers fisting his sandy strands.

"Oh god… mmm…" she moaned, clutching his head to her breast as the fog of pleasure descended.

Damn him!

Why did he have to be so good? How was she supposed to resist this young stud when just the feel of his mouth on her breast was enough to make her loins throb with liquid passion? "I ... can't ... oh god! Stick it in... fuck me! Fuck me with that big dick!"

Hugh, however, was in no hurry.

Licking the tip of her nipple, he slowly reached between her quivering thighs and slid a finger along her wet sex while gently circling her clit with his thumb. Low sounds flowed from her in heated breaths as her hips rolled wantonly against his touch. And taking that as his cue, he suddenly snapped her legs open. Hearing her surprised squeak, he grinned wolfishly around her breast before moving into position, the rounded crest of his cock sliding up and down her folds...

The sound rang out as loud and shrill as a banshee's wail.

Lost in the depths of her fantasy, it hit Elizabeth like a bucket of ice water.

Atop the bedside table, the digital clock was flashing, illuminating the time in bright red numerals. Its alarm sang its ear-splitting song.

Besides her, Patrick lurched awake.

"Oh shit, I'm late!" he barked, jumping up from the bed and gathering up his clothes from the floor.

Tangled in the bed's voluminous sheets, Elizabeth watched as her husband pulled his trousers up his legs and shoved his shirt down a waistband that visibly strained to contain his suety bulk before waddling out their bedroom.

Downstairs, the front door slammed shut behind him. His Alfa's V12 engine roared to life, its tires squealed, and there was a blast of a protesting neighbour's horn as he sped off down the street.

With a sigh, Elizabeth rolled over and silenced the cursed clock before falling back into the mound of pillows.

He didn't spare her so much as a backwards glance.

So, what else is new.

It was the same every time he had to go away on a sales trip. She'd like to say she was used to it, but the idea that he could just up and leave her without even saying goodbye left a very bitter taste in the back of her throat.

Had he ever even loved her? Had there ever been a chance for them?

Hot tears began to well at the corners of her eyes.

No, I won't cry! She told herself. *I won't cry for him. He's not worth it.*

For what felt like hours, Elizabeth toyed with the idea of going back to sleep. However, her body was trembling with unspent passion and before long the burning in her loins, that constant reminder of how close she'd come, drove her from her bed. Letting the sheets fall to the floor, she quickly donned her fluffy pink dressing gown before walking down the steps that led up to and from the master bedroom. Going through the hall and into the kitchen, she busied herself for a moment with the task of making a strong cup of tea before walking out into the back garden and breathing in the cool morning air.

It was hard to believe it was already October. Her garden was as beautifully vibrant as it had been in spring. The trees were still green. Everywhere flowers bloomed and birds sang.

Nothing was right, and yet it was all so perfect. So much like her own life.

And now, for another week, she was free.

It had been a month since that night. The night that had changed her life. A month since she had given into temptation, broken her marriage vows, and surrendered her body and soul to another man.

A month since she had taken Hugh Becket as her lover. Hugh, the boy she'd watched growing up, the young lawyer just coming home after years of living in the city. Hugh, her son's best Friend.

And the greatest fuck of my life.

Something had happened to her that night. Something that went beyond mere sex. He'd opened her eyes to a whole new world, given her a glimpse of something new and exciting. Something she'd never dreamed she was capable of. She wanted to experience it.

Her son, her precious baby boy, was all grown up and away at university. Her husband was never at home. This was a new day, a new start, and a new chapter of her life. She was free to find herself, to discover who she was. She would recreate herself, and she knew just where to start.

Going back into the house, she retrieved her brand-new laptop from its hideaway under the kitchen table and started it up. Entering the password that was guaranteed to be uncrackable, at least to her dear loving husband who hadn't remembered their anniversary once in all their years of marriage, she selected the pre-installed Word processor. The screen went white with the infamous white page.

What better way to reinvent herself than by creating her character in a book?

Sipping her tea, she considered the screen for a moment, then typed.

Confessions of a Trophy Wife.
By Liz Becket

The End...

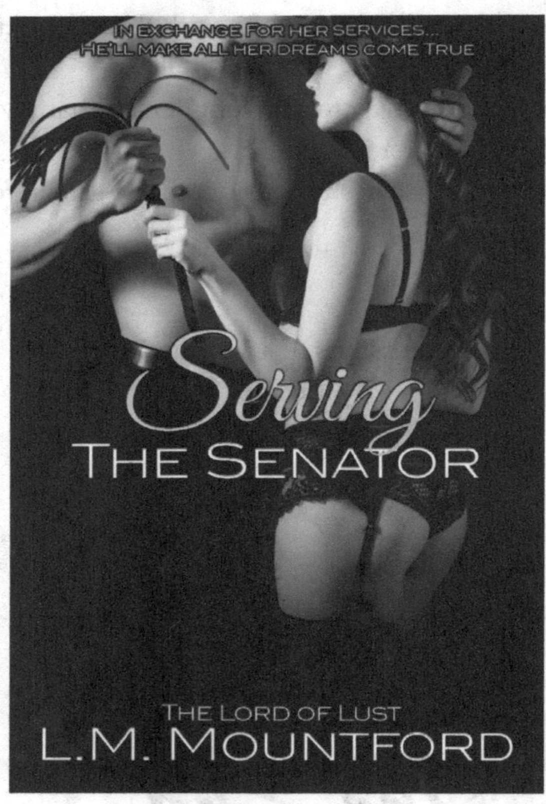

IN EXCHANGE FOR HER SERVICES...
HE'LL MAKE ALL HER DREAMS COME TRUE
Serving
THE SENATOR
THE LORD OF LUST
L.M. MOUNTFORD

Serving the Senator

Dom Diaries 4

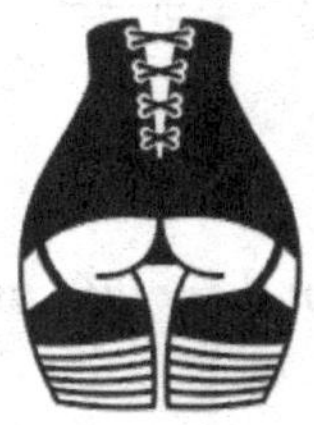

L.M. Mountford

Chapter One

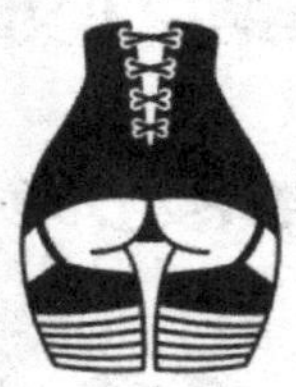

I stand before them, bare and unadorned, a sacrificial lamb for their lusts.

My world is black, the blindfold ensuring I can't see a thing, but I can feel them. Feel them arrayed around me, their eyes raking over me, devouring me from head to toe. Making my skin shiver with gooseflesh as the heat of their eyes burns across my breasts before licking down the flat of my belly to my…

I can hear them too. Their murmurs and bawdy jokes. I know I should feel insulted. They're acting like I'm some prize stud mare they're preparing to bid on. But the game is just too exhilarating.

I'm standing before them, naked and blindfolded, waiting for their command, and I love it.

I feel **him** coming up behind me.

He doesn't say a word, doesn't make a sound, but the sensation he always sends through me when he's near ripples up my spine, sending the pit of my belly into cartwheels. Then he's right behind me. So close, I can feel **it** nestling between my buttocks. I have to force myself to stay still, my heart fluttering like a robin redbreast in a cage.

"Don't move," he orders, his voice low so only I can hear, his breath curling over the skin of my neck, making my whole-body tingle. It is a very sexy voice, as deep and cultured as a lush red wine, and authoritative. The voice of a man who gives orders all day and expects them to be obeyed.

It sends tiny shocks of ecstasy rushing straight down to the hot slickness at my centre and makes my clit greedily throb for more.

I nod my understanding, then hiss a soft gasp, more from surprise than pain, as he slaps my ass.

"Don't move," he repeats, louder this time, emphasising every word so our audience can hear. The stinging handprint he leaves on my poor butt seems to burn deliciously in answer. A part of me wants to nod again, to push him and see how far he will go, but I don't. I remain still and obedient, compliant. Submissive.

His hands come up slowly, enveloping me from behind, the tips of his fingers sliding up my belly and over my ribs to cup my breasts. I whimper at the contact. Robbed of sight, my other senses seem heightened, making my already sensitive tits deliciously tender as he rolls and tweaks my stiff nipples.

I heard him chuckle as my back curls, offering up more of my not inconsiderable cleavage. Secretly, that mischievous part of me hopes he might punish me again. Perhaps bend me over and spank me in front of all these men.

He is subtler than that. Instead, he takes his time, plumping and kneading with just the right amount of attention and neglect to work my body into a heated frenzy that has me all but chewing my lower lip.

"Such a horny girl."

His tone is hot and hungry, much like the way his cock is pushing against my butt and smearing slickness along my thighs, and I know he is enjoying this as much as I am. He enjoys teasing, being in control while pushing his paramour to the brink and watching her writhe in delirious ecstasy.

So I writhe. Mewing soft kittenish sounds, I push back with a roll of my hips, grinding my butt along his length, the thick mushroom head sliding closer and closer to my burning cun-

"Kora… Kora! Are you listening?"

Chapter Two

Startled out of my thoughts, I looked up to see my supervisor standing over me, hands on her hips and watching me pointedly from behind her pearl mask.

Oh crap…

My belly did a triple summersault under that look. Though by no means unkind, in the few weeks I'd been working under her, Demeter had quickly set about ensuring I knew she was a woman not to be pissed about. Who would enjoy *punishing* any girl that forgot it.

And had, frequently.

Heat blossomed across my cheeks. I quickly nodded before looking down at my feet. "Yes Ma'am."

I always had difficulty meeting her eyes. She was just one of those women who could totally disarm you with a look and carried herself with the confidence of a woman who owned her sexuality. I was totally overwhelmed by her and couldn't help feeling totally inadequate whenever she was close. Against her cascade of lush chestnut-red curls, sharp angular features, intense blue-grey eyes and gorgeous 4"11' build that seemed made for her leather corset styled bustier, I was a plain Jane.

"Sure."

I could feel her gaze scorching my skin as she eyed me, clearly not believing my less-than convincing lie, and I could just imagine her long and immaculate eyebrow arching beneath the mother of pearl likeness of her namesake. God only knows how long she might have been watching me just standing here, lost in my own little world.

My stomach flipped again, winding itself into a tight little knot. This wasn't the first time she'd caught me daydreaming. I'd been warned before, but I couldn't help myself. It was this place, it practically oozed sex appeal- as did the clientele.

God, please don't let me get the sack…

I needed this job. Student loans, along with my parents' debts, had left me broke. I couldn't afford getting my ass thrown back onto the job market after only a couple of weeks.

To my surprise, she just sighed and shrugged, like I was a naughty child that just wouldn't learn a simple lesson. "Go attend to the gentleman at table 12."

I couldn't believe my ears. "Ta-table…*12?*" Just saying that had the heat licking out from my centre, making my knees shake and my already slick pussy purr.

Oh God, no! Not 12, I'm not ready for that.

"12," she reiterated, in a tone that could cow the God of thunder. "He's waiting."

It was the epic clash of ice and fire. The cool edge to her tone crashed over the warmth in my centre.

Nodding again, I darted around her, so desperate to be out of my alcove and her sight, before she changed her mind, that I only just caught myself as I stepped out into the main smoking room. The close call earned me a hissed *tisk* from Demeter. *Graceful,* I hastily remind myself.

A maiden of the Olympus club is always graceful, and ready to serve.

Set amongst the heights of Midtown's numerous high-rise buildings, the Olympus Club was New York City's best kept secret. The exclusive *Gentleman*'s club of the city's elite. The den of vice and skulduggery. A house that catered to any and every pleasure. There was just one rule. Discretion.

The patron's valued their privacy and the *secrecy* the Olympus Club assured. Any member or maiden, regardless of wealth or position, status or connections, discovered discussing Olympus, would immediately be branded 'excommunicado'.

The smoking room rang to the song of chinking of crystal, and soft girlish giggles.

It was a masculine place. The furnishings were all deep, rich, hard wood and leather. Leather so supple and deeply padded that the management liked to joke they should arrange a contest to test it against a baby's bottom and a Labrador pup's fur, just to see which was softer. Original Picasso's and Monet's, Van Gogh's, and one that looked suspiciously like a 'liberated' Da Vinci, adorned the timber panelling. However, the greatest hidden treasure was the 'trillion dollar' view overlooking the cityscape, commanding views across Times Square and all the way downtown.

It took every last ounce of my self restraint not to succumb to the lure of the floor to ceiling window that made up the smoking room's outer wall as I slid around the frolicking patrons. One little look and it was as if all of New York knelt at my feet. I dare say that was the idea. Nothing stroked the egos of the mighty more than being made to feel like gods.

If nothing else, it was a long way up from my parent's place in Washington Heights.

Dionysus, the barman, looked up at me as I approached the bar and presented me with a serving tray decorated with sterling silver filigree.

"N-number 12," I said, my voice still a little shaky at the prospect.

God, get a grip girl, he's just a man.

By the way he moved so expertly towards a specific bottle, I had no doubt he knew exactly what to serve each patron. Though a most impressive number of decanters and bottles stood at the ready, they were just a fraction of what the Olympus's cellar had to offer, and he filled a tumbler with scotch, adding just a single cube of ice.

If I didn't know better, I would have sworn there was just a hint of a smirk to his lips as he placed the glass on my tray. Then he returned to his station, so I put it out of my mind.

There was no point dwelling on such things. Dionysus was practically an institution at the Club, he knew all the stories, all the skeletons hidden away, and not just those figurative ones. He wouldn't say a thing, even if I called him out and asked what was so funny.

As if I didn't already know.

All around the smoking room, patrons of all ages and shapes sat in the high-backed armchairs like they had been poured into them. Outside these walls, these were the cream of the crop, the living embodiment of Mrs Caroline Astor's four hundred. Businessmen and actors, politicians and bankers, lawyers, financiers, landowners…old money and new. Within the Olympus Club however, and away from the prying eagled-eyed paparazzi, they could be true to themselves and embrace their more dark and primitive impulses.

Some drank. Some smoked. Some gambled, either with cards, or the lives of their employees, moving them as they would pawns on a chessboard. And some enjoyed the benefits of their personal attendants.

I only half saw them as I pass by, the clash of white on black amongst the crowd, a tangle of limbs, bodies writhing upon a bulging chair. Hair ruffled and cheeks flushed. The tailored garments they'd ensured were immaculate in front of the cameras, like peacocks presenting their tail-feathers, and that no doubt cost more than anything I could earn in a decade, carelessly dishevelled, with buttons undone, ties loosened, and other articles cast away while the culprit wiggled her fine derrière in his lap.

None of it was full-on sex. Even here, few members would be so brazened out in the open. Regardless, they made no effort to hide their activities as I passed by, the tray raised over my head and the silks of my *uniform* fluttering with every step.

Then again, why should they, I was only a maiden.

As the ancient gods would disguise themselves as men and women to walk among their subjects, to see but be unseen, so the maidens of the Olympus Club would dress as such. Our faces were hidden at all times by a half-mask of our namesakes and our bodies dressed in a uniform of half transparent silks that showed off as much skin as possible, while keeping the necessary parts covered. On the premises, we left our names behind. Here we were servants, the gods of old, who made the world and now live upon it solely to serve.

I am just a servant of the house. I fetch and serve drinks, but at least the money's good. And there are the fringe benefits…

Table 12 was called a table only out of courtesy. In fact, it was nothing more than a little square side table to one of the better armchairs. The occupant sat half-cloaked in shadow, eased back and reading a small leather-bound book with one hand. Unlike all the other members, he was dressed smart casual, forgoing his usual contemporary suits for a pair of khaki chinos and a crisp pale blue polo-shirt. The buttons were undone, just hinting at the chiselled muscles beneath in a way that made me long to explore that rugged physique.

Amongst this den of predators and alpha dogs, he was at ease and in his element. The top male, the only one with no need to prove himself.

Chapter Three

"S-Senator…" My voice trembled around the word. Just being in his presence affected me, put me on edge.

My breath caught in my throat as his eyes darted up to fix on me, scrutinising me.

The look immediately sent a hot shiver through my centre. At the same time, I quelled under his gaze, shrinking until I felt only an inch tall.

His penitent stare.

I'd seen that look before, dozens of times in fact.

His instakill. The devastating look he reserved for journalists that asked him ridiculous questions. It always made for damn good television, but I never thought I'd find *that* look directed at me. It was ridiculously hot.

Forcing a dry swallow that rasped my throat all the way down, I presented my tray to him. "Y-your drink, Sir…Scotch on the ro-"

"You're new." It wasn't a question, merely a statement of an obvious fact.

I nearly jumped out of my skin as his low growl thrummed through me. "Yes! I mean…Yes, Sir." I looked away, heat burning my cheeks- and other places further south.

Jeez, his voice couldn't sound any more made for fuckin' if it came with a side of strawberries and cream for dippin'.

He had the sexiest voice. Low and gravely but with a flowing command that had been forged on the playing fields of Eton or Oxford. The sort of voice that could inspire fear, demand respect, or reduce a poor, sex-starved girl to a puddle of wanton horniness with just a word. It was the voice in all my fantasies, the one I heard ordering me to cum for him.

Yet here he was silent.

Fighting to control the hot pulsing turning my knees to jelly, I slowly raised my eyes back up. He was still watching me, his eyes a hard icy blue, baleful and intense against the surrounding shadow. He was watching me, raking me from head to toe, studying me the way the wolf studied its prey, judging whether the meal would be worth the effort, before exploding into a run after the bunny.

He held my gaze for a moment, and I felt like he was looking into me, through me. Then he shifted, leaning forward so slowly I felt my breath catch as the shadow was peeled back.

Oh…My…God…

It wasn't a kind face. Nothing about Senator Richard Sharpe could ever be called kind. No, it was as hard and jagged as obsidian, a broad chunk of rock that a master mason had chiselled into a work of art. With that square jaw rough with stubble, sharp nose, wicked twist of a mouth, and raven black hair just that bit too long, he looked more like a soldier of fortune than a paper-pushing bureaucrat. And all the sexier for it.

I struggled to keep my nerve as his eyes raked over me with more interest than could ever be considered appropriate in the outside world.

But here, anything goes.

"Has anyone claimed you yet?" He asked it as calmly as he would enquire about the weather.

"What, no!" I exclaimed quickly, too quickly. "I mean, no Sir they haven't." Feeling the heat returning to my face, I placed the Senator's whisky on his table. "I'm not-"

"Such a waste." The Senator rose to his feet like a cobra rearing from the grass to loom over me.

So big…he never looked this impressive on TV.

Ignoring the drink I'd just laid down for him, he stepped around me, his eyes scorching lines of fire that seemed to burn through my already skimpy uniform as they took me in from head to toe again. Then he did the unthinkable, and gently touched his hand to the base of my back.

"Beautiful."

"Senator…I…I…" I stammered, not sure what to say, barely even able to form words. Fire and electricity crackled at his touch, raising a rush of gooseflesh where our skins touched. Lush heat ignited and pooled in my centre.

No this wasn't right. I couldn't let this go on. I mustn't. Club rules may be lax as far as the members were concerned, but for the staff, and in particular the maidens, they were very strict.

"You take good care of yourself." Another statement. His fingers brushed gently up my spine, then slid just under my ribs as he continued walking around me. My legs quickly turned to jelly under his scrutiny. I knew I needed to put some distance between me and this man, but my body refused to move as he stroked that place just below my left breast.

"I-I try, Sir," I forced out, my throat thick and uncooperative as I tried to restrain the moan that wanted to burst free as he drew closer and closer. "Please…Senator…I…"

To my surprise, and considerable disappointment, his hand suddenly dropped away and he slid back into his chair with all the panther-like grace with which he had arisen from it, before taking up his drink and holding it out to me. "Here. Drink with me."

"Oh! Err, no Sir, I'm not supposed to-"

"I wasn't asking." He dismissed my refusal by pressing the glass up to my lips. "Drink."

Fingers shaking, I accept the drink, sipping it cautiously. I wasn't much of a drinker, even on nights out I'd only stuck to the fruity, colourful, girly cocktails, and it was all I could do not to gag. The whiskey burned like fire all the way down, the taste strong but smoky and not at all unpleasant.

He watched me as I drank, the way a wolf watched a deer, observing, waiting for that one perfect moment to pounce. The look sent a throb of desire straight through my centre and I couldn't resist a second swallow before he pulled the glass away.

Raising it up to his mouth, he downed the hard alcohol and placed the tumbler back on the table.

This was my chance, I knew it, my chance to get away, but I was captivated by the sight of single drop of amber rolling down his chin and my body wouldn't obey my commands anymore. The sight of him brushing that drop of whiskey away with his thumb, then sucking the pad clean was the sexiest damn thing I've ever seen.

Forcing a dry swallow, I scrambled to regain my composure. "C-c-can I…I mean, will there be anything else, Sir?"

The Senator reached down and fingered the fastenings of his chinos. His eyes flashed like sunlight dancing on blue ice. "Mmm…Yes. There is just one more thing."

Chapter Four

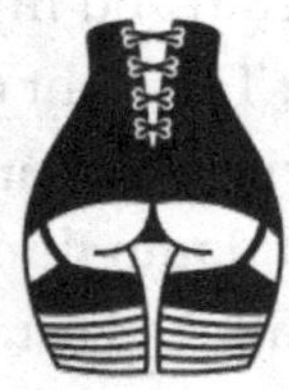

I averted my eyes, the sound of the zip cascading over me like ice water as I looked for something, anything that might otherwise require my attention. "I'll fetch you a girl."

"No."

My mouth felt drier than the desert. "Bu-but what am I-"

"I want you, Kora."

"Please *Senator*." My heart was beating so hard, I could barely speak. "I'm only a maiden. I'm not allowed to-"

"Are you talking back to me? Look at me!" His voice did not raise with the command, but the sudden delicious harshness was as dangerous as it was irresistible. My eyes swivelled obediently, the view that greeted me sending a spike through my centre to my clit. "I said, I want you. You did this to me, so it's only right you should attend to my *little* problem." Except, there was nothing little about his problem.

I did that?

There was at least six inches of stiff cock rising out of the fist curled around it's root and midsection, ending in a cut crown that was shiny with pre-cum and flushed a vivid purple.

I'm no virgin. I've seen my share of dicks, and learned to enjoy the bodies attached, but they had been mere boys.

Senator Sharpe was a man, with a man's cock. All ten inches of it!

The sight of it made me forget we were right in the middle of the most exclusive club in New York, surrounded by some of the richest, and most influential people in the world.

Sweeping my tongue across my dry lips, I reached out. Heat radiated off him, and I could practically feel his pulse pounding as I touched a finger to the place just beneath his broad crest. Jesus, he was hard, but also soft, like steel wrapped in warm silk. And hot, so fucking hot.

A good maiden should always attend to the members' needs…

"That's it, *Kora*…" That wasn't my name, not my legal name anyway, but the pained ecstasy in his tone, the sheer wanton restraint, had goosebumps rising all across my body and drew my gaze up to his. The heat in his eyes told me all. He wanted me. Wanted all of me, to possess and dominate. And he could take me. He knew I was his, whether I would admit it or not.

Holding his gaze, I bowed my head, his heady flavour spilling over my taste buds as I curled my tongue around that thick crown and took him into my mouth. However, the senator's only response was to arch his brow, that granite jaw locked in a silent challenge.

I gladly accepted. Heart pounding, I mouthed the plush head, sucking and drinking up the heady salty goodness of his pre-cum.

Still, he gave no outward sign, but I could feel the tension amassing within him, the pressure building as his cock grew thicker, harder within my mouth, so I decided to kick things up a notch. I sank to my knees between his. Placing both my hands on his trouser clad thighs, the muscles beneath bunching at my touch, I pivoted so he could see himself bulging against the inside of my cheek and dragged my mouth down the right side of his shaft, down to where his hand still grasped it, offering himself to me. I teased my tongue around the whitening knuckles, then came slowly back up his left flank before taking him into my mouth.

There was movement on the very edge of my vision, and it gave me a perverse thrill to know that the people around were starting to take notice. I glimpsed them nudging and gesturing, shifting to get a better view. They were attempting to be subtle about it but made little real effort to hide their interest.

I was beyond caring. I have always loved giving head. Loved the thrill of having so much power over people so much stronger than me and making them come undone. It was a potent mix, intoxicating. Swept along by the heat of the moment and drawn in the eroticism that the senator seemed to radiate, my only thought was on the task. I didn't care who saw, who watched. I wanted to beat this man, this titan. I wanted to shatter his control, break his willpower, and make him cum in my mouth.

I'd wanted to take him all in, but there was just too much of him. He was too big to deep throat- just the head seemed to fill my mouth to the brim- so I teased between going fast and slow, sucking him in as deep as I dared before pulling back.

"Oh *fuck*..." His, low, almost edgy groan was music to my ears and my neglected pussy pulsed and burned in wanton need as his fingers threaded through my hair, fisting and forcing me back down.

He held me there, his hips churning up, fucking my mouth with the savage intensity I had only ever fantasised about. Hot salty tears burned my eyes. I couldn't breathe, he was going too deep, had me forced down so far my nose was nestled in the nest of dark curls, but I couldn't have cared less.

Then I felt the rush of victory as with a ragged groan and a penetrating thrust that took him all the way into my throat, he came.

He came hard.

Unable to pull away with the Senator's white knuckled grip forcing me down, I sucked him greedily, drinking every hot creamy shot. I kept on sucking even after he had spilled everything he had to give, milking him for all he was worth.

"Mmm..." He purred, the hand falling from my hair to collar my throat. He forced me to abandon my new toy and pulled me up to look him in the eye. "That was very good." He was still hard but tucked himself back inside his chinos, his eyes dark and burning into mine with barely restrained lust. "But now it's time, Kora."

Chapter Five

The senator didn't offer any explanations as he led me, and I didn't ask.

Shame and embarrassment burned my cheeks. I could feel every eye in the lounge on me as we passed, but I didn't dare meet them. Not even when I glimpsed Demeter glowering at me, her eyes scorching trails across my back, down to where the large hand was moulding my buttocks. I was so getting fired for this.

Then he took me through the back door, into a small square foyer that housed a single elevator, the entrance to the underworld. It was a dark, unfurnished place with naked stone walls. Four life size sculptures etched from polished black marble stood sentry in each corner. They were impressive figures, taken straight out of the pages of Frank Miller's *300* and poised with swords raised and hoplites bared. Behind their helms, garnets had been set in the place of eyes and blazed in defiance. At the base of each, a plaque had been set upon a plinth, stamped with one of four legends in gold print – Penthos, Curae, Nosoi and Geras.

The elevator door slid open as we approached, the bright interior throwing long shadows across the floor. I blinked, the light blinding. The Senator held me close and guided me through. Yet the closeness was almost as disabling as the brightness. Awareness shivered up my skin and just the sound of his breathing had me coming out in goosebumps.

If the foyer was small, then the elevator was practically claustrophobic. A tiny space barely large enough for one with walls lined by plush red velvet. The only distinguishing feature was a brass control plate etched with the name *Charon* etched across the top and a row of buttons to reach the five floors above.

Under these was a scanner plate.

This was my first time going into the Underworld. It was the private area of the Olympus Club that only members and their personal attendants were permitted to enter. Unlike its name sake which had been believed to be on the edge and beneath the world of ancient Greece, Olympus's Underworld took up the floors directly above the club.

Senator Sharp removed a gold coin from his pocket and pressed it to the scanner.

"Where are you taking me?" I asked when the car began to rise, my heart pounding in my breast.

"Somewhere private. I have a proposition for you, Kora." He didn't look at me, but I could feel him watching me all the same. It made me feel hot, made my sex slick and tits heavy.

"Yes? What's that? Sir." I licked my lips, my mouth dry.

"Patience" He dismissed, the hand on my back starting to brush up and down the curve of my spine through my silks. *"All good things to those who wait."*

Up and down, up and down, getting lower and lower until his hand brushed under the folds of my uniform. I felt my legs start to tremble. Tingles shivered out from where skin touched skin, spiralling straight up to my poor, neglected clit.

I clamp my legs together, trapping his hand between them even as I rubbed my thighs together, desperate for some friction to quell the need raging down there.

"Open"

I had never enjoyed being bossed around, but the quiet authority in his tone made it feel so right, even as my body screamed in protest. I obeyed, splaying my thighs as far as they would comfortably go. Then his fingers took over, his hand cupping my greedy sex.

"Already so wet?" His tongue slid around the shell of my ear as one of his digits slid through my creamy folds to circle my clit. "Want more?"

"Please…" My tone was breathy, desperate and pleading. I couldn't stop myself from fisting his top and clinging to him for dear life as my legs almost gave way, the spike of pleasure from the contact going from my core to my fingertips.

"Please?" The senator asked, pressing down on my little bundle of nerves before drawing the finger back.

I bit back my protest, along with half a dozen sarcastic retorts. "Please…Sir-ohh!" As he pushed his thick finger into me, my mouth fell open in a low moan and his mouth crushed against mine.

It was not a soft kiss. It was hungry and violent. His mouth claimed mine, the silky softness of his tongue mirroring the strokes of his finger, delving inside me with an expertise that had my whole core tightening. It was too much. I couldn't stand it. Despite myself, my hips started to roll, my blood pumping fast and hot as the world started to spin around us and –

He pulled away as the elevator chimed, his finger slipping out of my heat and leaving me feeling woefully empty. Breathing hard, I leaned up on my tiptoes to follow, but the Senator just stepped around me, through the opening doors into…

Oh my god! It's Hades's Palace…

I'd thought it was just a joke. A gag to play on the F.N.G.s, (The *Fucking New Gods)*, but there it was.

The word was, it was a premium extra exclusive add on, that was available to only one member of the Olympus Club. None of the staff; maidens or even the attendants, knew which member it was, so most of them thought it was a myth, like most of the other stories they'd heard about The Underworld.

I couldn't believe it. Hades Palace, the secret, exclusive penthouse/ fuck pad was real!

Stepping out of the elevator, I seemed to move from the light into the Nightscape of New York City. Though no lights were on inside, the radiance of the city, and the full moon above glowed through the high windows and Balcony's French doors, giving it an almost starlit twilight.

It was too dark for me to make out much furniture, but I could tell what there was, was carved from polished black stone, as were the floor tiles and architecture. Everything was stone, except for the four-poster bed. A king-size of course, fitted with raven silk sheets and piled high with what could only have been the biggest, softest pillows I have ever seen.

I wasn't sure where to look, so instead I focused on the one familiar fixture of the room.

Senator Sharpe stood staring out across the city with his arms behind his back, like an emperor looking out across his domain. Or a god.

I approached him cautiously, suddenly so very aware of how large he was as his impressive build was framed alongside the spear of the empire state building.

"Do you ever take the time to just look at it?" he asked, still not looking at me.

"Umm…No"

"You should. It is a beautiful city by moonlight," he sighed. "I love this view. It almost makes the mercenary rates the management charge for this little place worth it."

"Well, I never have time to just stop and look."

"Shame."

"I have commitments, loans- student loans!" I quickly clarify, for some reason overcome by a need to explain, to make him understand. "And my mother's medical treatments-"

"I know. Second stage lung and throat cancer. Two different strains of cancer forming simultaneously is a very unfortunate coincidence." He pivoted to face me, and I felt my breath catch at the raw intensity in his eyes. "And costly."

I didn't say anything. I didn't even ask how he knew about my mom. Given the secretive nature of the Olympus Club, my contract included not just numerous nondisclosure agreements, but a legal agreement, stating my consent to an unspecified number of background checks a year. Of course, the details of such checks were supposed to be confidential, but it wasn't hard for me to imagine some of the more influential members being given brief peeks.

"What would you say if I told you your mother could be receiving a consultation from the best oncologist in the country? All expenses and treatment fully covered and free of charge."

"I'd tell you to stay on your meds. Goodnight." I wheel away, tears starting to burn in the corner of my eyes as the world started to spin. How dare he, no one uses my mother like that, no one!

"I can make it happen." He says after me. "This time tomorrow, she can be on a private jet. A consultation with Dr Leo Getts scheduled for first thing the day after tomorrow."

I didn't look back, not until I was in front of the elevator, my finger poised over the call button.

I wanted to, but I just couldn't bring myself to push.

He was shitting me. He had to be. It was just too good to be true. That sort of treatment, hell, just an hour's consultation would cost an arm and a leg, never mind the expense of crossing the country, and lodging, private nursing staff…Why would be willing to go through all that?

But what if he was on the level?

A single tear slid down my check as I turned back to face the senator, only to find him towering over me. I hadn't even heard him coming after me.

I bite back my surprised gasp. "Wh-what would I have to do?"

"Be my attendant." His arms cage me as he flattens both hands on the elevator, bracing himself as he bends forward, closing the gap so we were nose to nose, his eyes dark and hot.

"You're joking?"

He had to be. While attendants continued to receive the basic salary, the additional costs of their exclusivity and *services* were covered by their 'Masters'. The price, and terms, were negotiated between the two parties, and could sometimes even go so far as positions in real world jobs. But what he was offering went beyond generous.

"Never."

He more growled than said the word, and our closeness was so intoxicating I could practically feel it vibrating through me. "You're the only maiden I can trust.

They haven't had their claws in you yet, and they never will, if I claim you tonight. I need you, *Kora*."

His proximity and the raw intensity in his tone made it impossible for me to look him in the eye. "But you can't…I mean, maidens need a minimum of two years' service before they can be considered for a attendant. I've only been here a month…"

I was shaking, need and desperation had my blood running hot and thick through my veins.

He chuckled. "Yes, I know. Recommended by the Honourable Justice Lovejoy, the father of a university friend who you dormed with for a few months until you moved in with a local boyfriend. You remained friends with her but broke up with him after you found him in bed with his boyfriend."

The remark grounded me slightly, giving me a much-needed surge of anger that helped get a momentary grip of myself and wheel away from him to face the comforting cool steel front of the elevator. "You've done your homework. Do *they* have my bra size in their background checks too?"

"Anything's obtainable, Kora, even you." He whispered in my ear, before curving over me to sweep his tongue around the shell, his hands enfolding my waist. "And you never wear a bra."

Wound up tight in a knot of tension, I practically jumped out of my skin when, as if to prove his point, he cupped my right breast through my robe.

I won't lie, I've always had very nice tits, well rounded and perhaps a bit more generously proportioned than most woman with my build, but with absolutely no sag, and topped by dusky nipples that my lovers seemed to just love sucking.

For all my bountiful offering however, his hand completely covered my cleavage and I couldn't help my whimper when he plumped my breast.

"W-what if I refuse?" Almost beyond speech, I was panting with the words. *Touching…He's touching my…he shouldn't…I must – oh God…*

"You won't." He purred, rolling one of my tender nipples between his thumb and finger, their roughness exciting my skin through my robe.

"N-n-noo-oh!"

His musky scent was everywhere, all around me, fogging my brain and invading my thoughts. Damn, he smelt so good.

"No, you want what I'm offering." He took my left hand in his and guided it down to the crotch of his trousers. My core tightened and throbbed at the feeling of his renewed hard-on straining against the fabric. "It's all yours for the taking. All you have to do is say *yes…*"

Then he spun me around to face him and took my mouth before I could form a word.

It was all aggression and heat. Not so much a kiss as a claiming. I whimpered as his tongue found mine, stroking me with lush coaxing licks that had me melting against him as my damn needy pussy purred with delight. In the next instant, his arms were around me, his hands curling around my waist, grabbing my butt and crushing me against the wall of hard virile male, making me feel how *hard* he was.

I needed to be strong. I knew it. This was my chance, I had to stop, had to pull away or slap him or knee him, or, or just, something…

Anything…

Anything but grab his hair and return the kiss, my spine curling up so he could feel my cleavage push against him, one leg sliding up his, coiling round his-

Oh God. No, no! I had to push him away. Push him away now before it was too late.

But I couldn't. It was all too much for me. He was too much for me.

My pussy was hot, my breasts heavy and tender with nipples that just ached to for attention, and all I could think about was that this was Senator Richard Sharp. The Senator Richard Sharp. The man I had been crushing on since I saw his first ever televised political debate, and he was kissing me.

No, he wasn't kissing me. His mouth was basically fucking mine, and I loved it.

Somewhere in a distant, still coherent corner of my mind, I could feel him guiding me backward. I didn't resist. Rather, I practically climbed up him, my legs coiling around his waist, hips gyrating against the bulge of his dick as he took me deeper into the room, until he had me pinned against one of the his massive fourposter's beams.

My whole body shivered deliciously at the feeling of being cornered by this big alpha male, overwhelmed by the feeling of his massive cock sliding along my slit through our mesh of clothes. It was the most divine torture. The barrier teased me by preventing any real depth, while the mix of textures rubbing over my tender tissues drove me wild. God, he felt so good. So big. So-it wasn't enough.

I needed more of him.

"Mmm… say it, Kora." The senator growled, pulling back just enough to break the kiss, before he buried his face in the crock of my neck.

"I shouldn't." He sucked hard on my pulse spot, making me gasp as desire shot through me. "I mustn't…please!"

"Please what?" he growled again, setting me down on legs that shook like jelly as he nipped trails of fire.

I whimpered, shaking my head, my body hot and thrumming like a taught violin string.

Oh God…Oh God! This can't be happening. This can't be-

"Say it!" His hands encircled my wrists, raising them up above my head before pressing them to the timber post.

"Yes!" I couldn't stop the flood. His words, the way he held me, pinned me to his bed and devoured my very being. It was too much. "Yes. I want more. You can have me however you want, I'm all yours. Just give me more."

Chapter Six

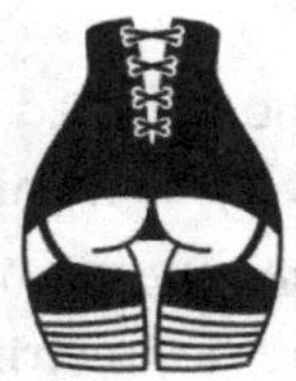

"Good girl," he praised, and gave my ear lobe a long suck, before drawing back. "Now, don't move."

The command sent a shiver through me, its gruff, no-nonsense tone echoing the voice from my fantasises. I obeyed.

His face impassive, the Senator collared both of my wrists in one of his hands, before reaching for something out of my line of sight. Heat rushed through me when he raised what it was up for me to see.

Dangling, between his thumb and forefinger, was a red silk scarf.

Oh God, where did that come from?

"Don't move,' he repeated, and the thrill it gave me to hear that lush commanding tone had me biting my lip in anticipation.

It wasn't just a command. This was a test. He was daring me, baiting me to test the boundaries of this new role.

I was his attendant now. I must obey his every command immediately and without hesitation, or I'll be punished.

And in return, he'll take care of all of mom's medical bills.

He swept the scarf around my wrists once, tied off, then repeated the tie around the bed post. It wasn't anything as secure as handcuffs, but the silk was much kinder to my skin and a testing tug from the senator proved I wouldn't be getting away any time soon.

He took a moment to admire his handiwork.

"Mmm…Very good, Kora," he purred. Awareness rippled up my spine and I felt my skin rise with goosebumps as he trailed a finger down the underside of my right arm. "You're mine now. You're going to have to do everything I say."

I nodded, my heart racing as his finger trailed down my silks to the swell of my breasts, my nipples standing unashamedly against the fabric.

"I do mean *everything*, Kora."

"Yes Master-oh!" I couldn't help my kittenish gasp when he cupped the swell of my left breast and thumbed the tip. "Mmm…Give it to me, please…do anything you want to me, I'm yours."

"Yes, you are." he breathed, squeezing my cleavage through my garment, the warmth of his touch bleeding through the silk to lick my skin. "But you have to earn your place as my attendant."

"Yes, make me earn it." It was the sweetest torture. My body hummed with tension and the need to move, to arch and offer myself to him, to force his hand to where I needed it, was almost overwhelming. Damnit, I had to resist.

Don't move. Just don't move, you can do this, you can…

"You'll beg for it." His eyes flashed at the promise.

Despite my resolve to obey, when his thumb and finger closed around my nipple and twisted it, it was all too much.

"Yes!" My head rolled, the moan flowing from me in painful ecstasy as my spine curled.

Even his softest touch sent fire and electricity through my core.

"Kora." His tone was clipped, disapproving. "I told you, don't move. I see I'm going to have to teach you obedience."

"I-I'm sorry Master. It won't happen again."

"I know." The Senator gave my nipple another twist, this time a little harder. Not enough to hurt, but enough for me to know. Then his hand was moving again, fingers brushing over the swells of my bosom, beneath the folds of silk to the bounty of naked skin, and down. Down the valley of my breasts. Down the flat-plain of my belly. And down to the string of well-sodden fabric that was all that covered my throbbing sex.

"I've been a bad girl. Very, very bad, teach me to be good. I'll do any…anythi- oh God!"

He cupped my pussy through my panties, his middle finger sliding through the outline of my swollen folds to press down on my clit. I was so sensitive, that that little contact set off supernovas behind my eyes.

I couldn't take it. I had to touch him. I needed to grab him, feel the muscles rippling under his skin and lust pounding in his chest. I couldn't bare it, except the scarf held me fast and wouldn't loosen, no matter how much I twisted and tugged against it. All I could do was claw desperately at the timber as he traced the line of my sex through my panties with a maddening softness that made my skin tingle and feel too tight.

"You're soaked. What am I going to do with you Kora? You must really be gagging for it.".

"Yes, I – I need it Master. Give it to me, I want it, I want it." My hips rocked into his touch, desperate to steer his attentions back towards my little bundle of nerves. Fuck, I didn't care if I sounded like a wanton slut. I didn't care at all.

He took me and made me forget my inhibitions.

With a look, he'd made me forget all my determination not to fall into such a role. A word from him had reduced me into a steaming mess of sexual frustration. And just a touch had me on the verge of losing my mind. Fuck, I was so close, just a little more, that's all I needed. Just a little more and I would cum all over his fingers.

"Good girl, you're being much more honest now. But still so disobedient," he chuckled, lowering his head until we were almost nose to nose. "It wouldn't be a punishment if I just gave you what you wanted now, would it?" Hooking his finger under my underwear, he quickly pulled it aside.

I moaned, shaking my head even as I strained to reach him, offering my lips to him in open invitation. "N-no…"

It's hard to say whether I was agreeing with him or protesting.

Either way, I watched wide-eyed as the senator made a show of bringing his wet and shiny finger up to his lips and sucked it clean. "Mmm…you're delicious."

I lost all control at that. My core clamped down in wanton spasms while my hips bucked and my body started to tremble. I was so tight with sexual tension, one good pluck would have me twanging like a guitar string "Oh God, you're such a tease."

"Yes, and you love it."

"I love it." I could practically feel his lips brushing over mine, so close, just one more inch.

His hand cupped the nape of my neck, then his mouth was back on mine, swallowing my moan as his finger pushed inside me.

He started slow, with just that one *thick* finger hooked forward to stroke the place behind my clit, the broad pad deliciously rough against my delicate tissues. It stirred me into a frenzy as he pushed the digit back and forth, somehow managing to keep perfect rhythm with his tongue so the dual stimulation worked to maximum effect.

Whoever said men couldn't multitask had obviously never been finger banged by Senator Richard Sharpe.

"Remember. Don't. Move," he growled against my mouth in that hot authoritative tone, emphasising each word as a second finger pushed into me and sent me spiralling.

"I-I can't! I – I- oh fuck- I'm cumming!" I couldn't resist it. My orgasm washed over me like a wave on the rocks and had me arching in his arms, straining against my bonds in violent bucking tremors of ecstasy.

"Oh? You bad girl," he chided, dragging kisses along my jaw and down my neck. "You know you're going to have to be punished for this?"

I couldn't think. My world was shattering as I rode his fingers, the waves rushing over me, growing more powerful. Then his thumb pressed into my clit and I went wild. "Oh fuck! Yes! I'm such a bad girl…mmm…punish me…Master!"

"Oh…I will, later, but for now…" The hand on my neck moved down to the base of my spine, half supporting me and half pulling me against him as he bent down, his lips catching my right nipple and sucking.

His thumb rolled over my clit while he pushed his fingers in and out, in and out, working me into a frenzy. Helpless to resist, all I could do was writhe, throwing my head from side to side, clawing the post as heat and ecstasy radiated through from my core, out to my fingers and toes.

He pulled his mouth away, his eyes dark and burning up at me as he tongued my nipple through my silks and bore down on my clit with his thumb. "You just keep cumming, and so easily, you really have been gagging for it, haven't you, Kora?"

I was melting in his arms, the very fibre of my being turning to liquid and running down my thighs as my hips pumped greedily onto his fingers and thumb, sensation amassing in my core. "It's not…not my fau-oh fuck! I can't help it, you just…"

He licked his way back up my neck, his breathing quick and hungry with lust. "What do I do to you? Go on, say it Kora."

"You just keep making me cum!"

"Mmm…Good girl, now look into my eyes…"

I obeyed.

I would always obey. No matter what he wanted, I was his. He could have anything. For him, I would do anything.

"Cum for me Kora, cum all over my fingers!" His words were hot against my lips and the intensity in his kiss as he took my lips made my mind go blank.

"Please…no more…I can't take it anymore…" I panted when my brain started working again, and the blood stopped roaring in my ears.

He'd made me cum so hard, every muscle in my body felt like jelly and I didn't have the strength to stand. If it wasn't for his arm around me, I think I might very well have collapsed.

"Oh, my dear, sweet, innocent little Kora, I'll never stop." The dark promise in his tone sent renewed shivers through me, but then his fingers slipped from my heat and I was left feeling empty, and somehow even hornier as he brought the fingers to his mouth and licked them clean. "God, you just keep cumming but you're still so tight, this is going to be better than I thought."

Somewhere very, very deep down and far away, a mousy voice in my head asked what he meant, but I was too far gone to care.

He lowered me to the floor, so I sat propped again the bed, the silk tie sliding down the polished beam with me. When he straightened, I found myself staring at his covered cock. Somehow, even confined by his chinos, it looked larger than before, and was clearly visible as a massive bulge straining against the length of his right thigh.

I licked my lips hungrily and leaning forward, mouthed him through his trouser leg. When I traced the curve of his crown with my tongue, he made a strangled sound in the back of his throat. "That's it. Such a dirty girl…"

I nodded, much too eagerly. "Yes, I'm a dirty girl, Master. Your attendant. Let me serve you. I need it…I can't wait any longer…"

"But you will," he ordered, his lips pressed firmly together as he looked down at me, like a teacher preparing to punish a disobedient student. "You're mine now Kora, my attendant, my little toy."

I swallowed, the very thought of it making me bite my lower lip in anticipation. "And I have to do everything you say."

"Yes."

The chinos were undone with a quick movement of his hands and his renewed erection surged upward to stand tall before my eyes, it's length thickly veined, the head slick and flushed with colour. With one hand, he angled his dick down to point at my mouth. "So, attend to me."

I didn't need to be told twice.

I sucked him in greedily, taking him in as deep as I could, moaning as his salty goodness spilled over my tongue. His cock felt even more amazing in my mouth the second time around, and the way he watched me going down on him, with those eyes dark with lust, only made it that much hotter. I returned the gaze hotly as I pulled back to his crest then pushed forward again, watching with rapt attention as he pulled his top over his head to reveal a glorious bounty of male perfection.

I drank him in and wanted nothing more than to reach out and run my nails down that broad chest of defined muscle, his light dusting of course black hair seeming only to add to his appeal. Strange, I'd never really found chest hair to be attractive, but on him it only added to his allure. It made him look wild and untamed, and contrasted so vividly with the image of control he portrayed on the pages of GQ.

He was everything I'd ever imagined and so much more.

Spurred on by his little strip tease, I sucked harder, my cheeks hollowing as I drew him in. There was no fancy tricks this time. I just went all out and worshiped his dick with my mouth.

Then his hand slid though my hair, fisting and twisting, holding me still as his hips started rolling.

"Yeah…let your master fuck your mouth," the Senator groaned in a guttural rasp that sent a shiver straight down to the still heat between my legs. "Get me nice and wet for your tight little cunt."

His hips churned, the circles growing larger, forcing me to take him deep, deeper than I'd ever taken a man before.

This was new territory for me. Whenever I'd given head before, I'd always been the one in charge. It was all part of the thrill, but the senator somehow took that control away. Now he had the power and I gave in to his commands like a good attendant.

And I loved it.

He fucked my mouth hard, but with perfect control, his pace unwavering. I could feel him passing through the gate of my throat, the crown pulsing and swelling, and it made me crazy with need, desperate to feel him between my legs, filling me up-

He pulled back, withdrawing completely from my mouth. Then his arms were around me and he'd pulled me back to my feet, into a deep lush kiss that had me melting all over again. This was the first time anyone had ever kissed me straight after I'd sucked them, and the idea that he must be able to taste himself, was so kinky, I almost came.

And while his mouth took mine, his hands brushed up my arms to where I was manacled to the bedpost. Much to my embarrassment, the tie came undone with a quick tug. However, I had no time to enjoy my freedom, as no sooner had the silk come away than he was spinning me around, pushing me up against the post.

I clung to it gratefully, my legs still a bit too shaky. Smooth and polished to a high shine, the timber felt deliciously cool against my overheated skin. "M-Master, please!"

"Patience, Kora. You really need to learn patience, if you want to be my attendant." His low promise had me tingling all over, as did the way his hands slid down my back and under my silks to the string of my panties.

The delicate fabric snapped like dental floss under his huge hands. Then he hiked my silks up and over my butt and nudged my legs open further with his knees.

I obeyed and leant forward more, raising my ass in the air. I should have been embarrassed, knowing he could see *me*, all of me, my most private and personal places, but I wanted him to see.

"Ahh!" I gasped as he gave my backside a swat.

It hurt, a little, but then the sting dissolved into hot pleasure and I couldn't resist giving a quick inviting wiggle. Fuck, what was wrong with me. I'd never been into spanking before. Hell, I was acting like a complete slut, and I didn't care. The Senator was everything my dreams and fantasies had promised, and I just knew he was going to be so much more before he was finished with me.

"Like that Kora?" the Senator asked, slowly rubbing the hot spot his hand had left across my right cheek, massaging the heat into my skin. "Want more?"

Somewhere, there was the soft sound of a draw opening and closing. Then a packet tearing. But I was too consumed by the wantonness rippling through me to give it much thought. It just felt so good, I just couldn't stand it. "Yes!"

He withdrew his hand, letting the warmth bleed away. "Yes?"

I could feel him. Feel it. Feel its heat licking up my folds before its blunt tip pressed into my little bundle of nerves and fireworks sparked behind my eyes. I edged back, raising my hips to try and slide onto him, only for him pull back.

For a long moment, there was nothing. It was as if time held its breath for us and the sudden solitude of the moment made my heart thunder in my ears. And I was too scared to move, too breathe, in case all this shattered around me and revealed itself as nothing but just another incredible dream.

Then his mouth was by my ear, his voice a rumble that had my pussy clenching.

"Yes what?"

"Master!" I wailed, pleading. He'd driven me mad and I was just too horny to care. In all my life, nothing had ever gotten me this worked up. I needed him inside me, to feel his hardness filling me up. "Please Master…my cunt's so wet for you…give it to me…please, give it to me-oh oh God, oh fuck-"

There was pleasure, a sudden rush of sensation that spiralled out to my fingers and toes, but there was also pain. First there was a potent and very fiery bite, then a deep satisfying burn that made me ache for more as he slid into me, the wide crest parting my folds, stretching my delicate tissues and spreading me open, then pushing inexorably into my heat.

"Look at me, Kora."

I threw a desperate look back at him, my mouth dropping open in a long voiceless cry as he filled me, that first thrust splitting me open and driving into my core. Fuck, I could barely breath through the feeling. None of my previous lovers had prepared me for this. He was just too much.

"Mmm…you pull that sexy face when you're getting fucked and your pussy's so snug," he purred, grinning down at me as he continued pressing forward, with just the perfect amount of force, until he seemed to have gone as deep as he could go. "Just like fucking a virgin."

Heat flushed through my body, and I wanted to beg him not to say such dirty things, but I couldn't get the words out. Then one of his hands was cupping my nape and urged me down until I was bent at the waist, opening me up as he withdrew.

He drew back slowly, leaving me with a growing feeling of emptiness as he pulled out, until just the head remained inside me. Then he pressed in again, his hips snapping forward, and my head rolled back in agonising bliss.

"So-so big…I can't…too-too much…" I panted, my nails scouring the timber of the frame. This new angle had him stimulating a whole load of new nerves I had never felt before and he was so deep inside me, I could feel him throbbing through the rubber.

"You can, Kora. And you will," he promised, his dark and cultured voice growing ragged with passion. He repeated the move again, sliding out then thrusting back into me, then again, and again, building to a rhythm as his other hand on my hip began pulling me back to meet him.

Each time he went a little deeper. Working inch after inch inside me, until I felt like I was going to burst and was on the verge of going out of my mind.

My body however only craved more and pressed back to meet him, my greedy sex convulsing and throbbing, wrapping around him and sucking him in. "M-Master!"

The Senator chuckled at my plea, the sound so very gruff and primal, his hips slapping wetly against my butt as he made me take him even deeper. "Mmm…you feel so good, Kora, your pussy was made for my dick," he declared, like a captain claiming a newly discovered land.

"Y-y-yes that's your pussy…oh my god, yes! My little pussy is all yours Master. Oh fuck, it's yours…use me…make me take my master's cock…make me take it…take it…take it-oh!"

The mini orgasm swept through me hard and fast when he finally made me take him all and his wide crest struck *that* place deep inside me. He didn't let me rest or come down from the high, but fucked me through my release, circling his hips in tight little rolls as my walls clamped down around him and refused to let go.

I absorbed everything he had to give me, savouring every thick and gloriously hard inch of him, and craved more. Then his arms were around me, cradling me, drawing me back against him and driving me down onto his cock.

He was in complete control, my master in name and body, and I'd never dreamed someone, anyone, could dominate me so completely. I let him take me, my hands falling to my sides, fisting and balling against the pleasure while my head rolled back onto his shoulder as each curl of his hips drove me up onto my tiptoes.

"Oh God…oh God, you-you're going to make me cum again…"

I could feel *it* building, a hot throbbing knot in my centre and I pushed down, grinding against his cock, suddenly just needing to reach that peak. "Master, I'm gonna cum all over your dick…please…plea-!"

"You're gorgeous, Kora," he husked in my ear, his hands moving over me, touching and feeling, fanning the flames of my desire. Gathering up my silks, he dragged the garment from me and cast it aside before one of his hands came up to cup my left breast, plumping it while his thumb teased over my hard nipple. "Now…touch yourself."

"Master?" I gasped, breathless and close, so close that my legs were shaking with it. I was on the edge. I just needed a little more.

"I want you to make yourself cum, Kora."

"Master, please, I don't…I can't…it's embarrassing…" I pleaded, shaking my head even as his free hand took mine, and put it over the throbbing heat at my centre.

"Cum," he ordered, and I couldn't resist. There was something so illicit and sexy about the feeling of being skin to skin with the senator. It made me feel wild and desperate and I rubbed my clit, fast and hard, three fingers thrumming over the little bud as he continued driving in me from behind.

"That's it, cum for me Kora, cum for your master."

The dual cocktail of pleasures ignited a firework in my brain, and I stilled as the pleasure-shock of it washed over me, shaking me to my core in a delicious whiteout of sensation. And when I came down from the heights, I found myself stretched out across the bed with Senator Richard standing over me.

Breathing hard, my whole being a mass of tingling aftershocks, I could only watch in awe as he loomed over me. He looked so huge and great, so much more than flesh and bone. Like a god.

He was my Hades.

I'd played the role of a goddess, bound and chained for the service of mortals. He'd freed me. He'd freed me, unchained me and taken me to the underworld, his dark realm where he'd brought out all my forbidden and secret desires. Now I was his.

His attendant. His servant.

His Kora.

He didn't say a word. Just pushed his trousers down his long legs. I didn't know when he'd removed his shoes and socks, and I didn't care. I just knew what he wanted and obediently opened myself to him, my eyes riveted to his cruelly handsome face as he came for me, crawling up the bed until he was between my legs

"Mmm…such a sweet little cunt," he purred, bowing his head down to inhale the scent of my sex. "I've wanted to eat this pussy since I first set eyes on you Kora."

The feeling of his breath wafting over my sex sent a hot shiver of desire straight through me. "Master, I-"

He dragged his tongue up my folds, making my hips jump and I moaned a long sweet sound, before his mouth descended on my swollen and tender clit. He sucked with an intensity that had me clawing at the sheets, my body instinctively twisting away, desperate to escape the too-fierce pleasure of his mouth.

"Stay still," he growled, the low thrum of his words vibrating through the place our bodies joined and straight to my core.

"Oh, God!" My head rolled as his hands wound around my legs, cupped my ass and pulled me against his mouth. "Master…please…put your dick back in…I need it…plea-oh! Oh my god!"

He thrust his tongue inside me, deep inside me, and lashed my inner walls with twirling swirls that quickly sent me spiralling.

I was going to cum again.

I couldn't stop it, the multiple orgasms he'd already lavished upon me had left me raw and sensitive, too sensitive. And the image of his eyes, dark and smouldering, watching me from between my legs was just too much. I couldn't stand it. I couldn't-

I couldn't fucking believe it.

I wanted to scream and beat the bed as he reared back, leaving me hanging on the edge. "N-no! Don't…stop…"

Instead, he caged me with his body, that sinful mouth pressing to mine as the full weight of his desire settled against me. He kissed me for a long moment, his wily tongue resuming its sinful dance, working me into a breathless frenzy before he pulled back just enough to drink in the sight of me stretched out beneath him.

What a sight I must have looked.

When he touched my mask, I didn't resist. Nor did I try and stop him when he pulled it from me, but nor could I meet his eyes. I'd seen the pictures on social media and google. I knew the sort of woman Senator Richard Sharp liked. I didn't match up.

He liked blonde super models with delicate features and plenty of ass. Not raven-haired, doe eyed bookworms that made Hermione Granger look like Lara Croft.

I was realistic, I knew the score, but even so, I couldn't bare to see his look of disappointment.

"Look at me, Kora." Cupping my chin, he angled my head to look up at him. My mouth was dry by the time I met his eyes, their depths almost black with lust. There was no disappointment there. No rejection. Just want. "You're so beautiful, don't ever let anyone tell you different."

Still looking deep into my eyes, he thrust forward.

I gasped a voiceless cry, my back arching at the feeling of him surging inside me, filling me and pushing me back into the sudden rush of a mini-orgasm. It swept through me hard and fast and I was still shaking as he began rolling his hips, pulling back then thrusting home. It wasn't fast, but nor was it slow. It was firm, and steady, and pushed the sensations coursing through me on and on.

I was enslaved by the vision of him above me, his arms braced on either side of me, his muscles moving beneath his skin, bunching and tensing and powering the relentless draw and thrust of his hips. I watched him in awe, unable to tear my eyes from the sight of his dick sliding in and out of my sex, the condom stretched tight and shiny with my creamy desire.

He was a work of art. A machine built with the sole function of fucking me into oblivion.

"Mmm…no one's ever fucked you like I do, have they Kora?"

"No…not like you…no one…oh my god…" My hips churned as I tried to match him, my feet slipping and sliding on the silken sheets as I fucked him back, until he seized both my legs and raised them up onto his shoulders, opening me up completely I could feel him reaching my stomach. "Oh my god…feels so good…so fucking good and deep…I'm all yours Master, your little slut…I'm your good, little, slutty attendant!"

"Yes, you are Kora. Mine. All mine." He reinforced his ownership with each deep thrust, the delicious friction of it igniting a fire in my head that was melting my mind.

"I just want to be yours. Your good little toy…use my body to make your dick cum…I'm just here to please you…take me however you want…I'm yours-oh fuck-I'm all yours!"

And I was. I was his toy, ready and willing to do whatever he wanted, whenever he wanted me.

"Oh fuck-oh fuck- Master," Orgasm after orgasm began pouring through me, coming on so fast and hard, I could barely tell where one ended and the next began. "It's too-too much…I can't, can't stop cumming!"

"Yeah! That's it, Kora," the senator groaned, his head dipping down to nip and suck at my tingling nipples. "Keep cumming for me baby, milk my dick with your greedy little cunt."

The Senator was getting close too. I could feel it in the way his once measured thrusts began to quicken, as if he was racing to get me off just one more time.

So I bared down on him, fighting the terminus of my ceaseless orgasms to wrap my inner walls around him, wanting nothing so much as I did at that moment to make him blow. I wanted to see the pleasure twist him. I wanted to feel all his passion and desire flow through me. I wanted to know that I'd done that to him, reduced the most powerful man in New York City to a sweaty sated mess. I wanted-

"Oh fuck, here I come!" he rasped, gritting his teeth, momentarily trying to fight the stirring in his balls as he pulled out of me. Without my Master inside me, I felt cold and empty, but then he was on top of me and I forgot all of that. The Senator tore the condom off before fisting himself as he angled the red throbbing crown to me. "Open."

I did as I was ordered. And like the Persephone of ancient times, who ate the apple seeds offered by Hades and was so bound to the underworld for all eternity, I leaned up, took him in and drank down everything he had to give me.

He came hard, the hot salty build up filling up my mouth and running down my chin as I sucked him through it, his low rasping grunts and moans music to my ears. When he'd shot his third and final load, I licked him clean, swirling my tongue around his throbbing crest then up and down his shaft. I didn't miss a drop, like the good little attendant I was.

Only when I was certain he was clean did I pull off and promptly collapsed back into the warm embrace of the wonderfully cool silk sheets.

I couldn't remember the last time I'd felt so tired.

My eyes felt so heavy, and the world grew hazy as the aftermath of the most amazing sex of my life settled over me. I needed to sleep, just for a few hours

"Kora."

My eyes snapped open, suddenly wide awake. "Master?"

He grinned down at me, one of his massive hands coming down to stroke my hair as his dick stood to attention an inch from my nose. "Patience Kora, the night's still young, and I have a lot to teach you about Serving the Senator…"

The End

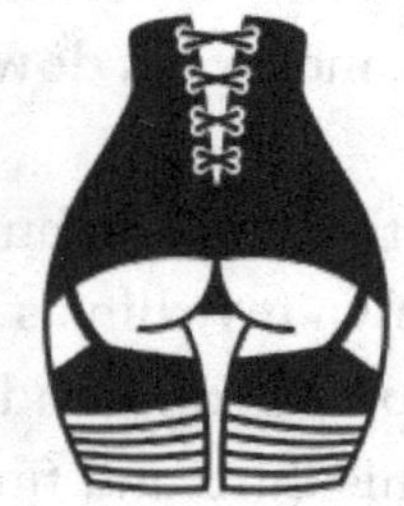

Sweet
Temptations:
THE BOSS'S DAUGHTER
THE LORD OF LUST
L.M. MOUNTFORD

Sweet Temptations:
THE BOSS'S DAUGHTER

L.M. MOUNTFORD

Prologue

His back burned and the spray cut clean to the bone as fat wet snakes slithered down his arms and legs, so cold they burned.

Eyes hooded and vacant, Richard watched the run-off collect around the shower drain, swirling around and around. The blood was almost washed away, leaving only long accusing fingers of dark crimson streaking across the porcelain.

Time had lost all meaning. Seconds and hours bled together until…

"Goddamnit!"

He wanted to scream. To shout. To bellow like a bear in a cage, being dragged through the streets for the amusement of a medieval mob, roaring and bawling in a show of futile outrage at the hard, inescapable reality. Yet the pitiful grunt was all he dared with Alexander in the next room, liable to stir at the smallest sound, and Alice sleeping peacefully just across the hall. So instead, he took it out on the shower wall the way an angry child would beat a pillow.

Red-hot knives stabbed between his knuckles and up his arm in a blast of near-crippling agony as he hit the wall hard enough for bone to crack against the porcelain. Regardless, he ground his knuckles into the tile, relishing the agony it induced, needing it and not knowing what else to do.

Then the moment was gone, and Richard was left shivering in the cold, hot tears stinging his eyes. "Wh-what the fuck have I done?" The question rang hollow, even to his ears.

What had he done? He'd fucked his babysitter, a girl almost young enough to be his daughter. He'd cheated on his wife. And, what was worse, he'd loved every fucking second of it. Then he'd fled.

He could still hear Rebecca crying in her room.

Her sobs had chased him out of the Blaire's flat like a pack of hounds snapping at his heels and it had been all he could do to make it back to the flat without breaking his neck. Alice had already gone to bed when he came bursting through the door. Deep down, a more rational part of him was relieved he didn't have to explain to his instinctively suspicious wife why he was getting in so late, or the fact he smelt like sex and his shirt was misbuttoned, but in that moment, all he could think about was a shower. He'd barely spared a moment to look into their bedroom to check on her before jumping into the bath and cranking the water temperature as low as it would go.

Goddammit! What the fuck had he done! Why had he even gone to fix the computer in the first place? It wasn't a vital job. Rebecca might have been in a state, but it could have waited until morning. So, why the fuck had he gone to the fix the bloody computer, when he'd known, he'd just known it was a bad idea.

Alarm bells had gone off the moment Alice had suggested the girl fancied him. He would have pressed her for more, but then she kissed him, and his world had dissolved to just the feeling of her luscious body pressing into his.

It had been much the same the night they first met, when she'd cornered him in The Burning Book's storeroom. He'd been getting a fresh crate of beer when he'd noticed her leaning against the door. He hadn't noticed her slipping in after him, and the sight of the tiny brunet, all curves and smiles in a black wrap-around dress that could only have been painted on, standing there with her hand on her hip almost had him jumping out of his skin.

Only the Lord alone knew how he managed not to drop the bottles in each hand.

Her smile had only grown more sinful when he'd told her she was in a staff-only area. Then, with a cock of her head and a pouting moan, she'd been on him and he'd promptly forgotten all of his fears of getting caught.

Richard would have stayed. He would have, but then Alice's remarks about Rebecca rung in his ears.

Suddenly, he couldn't get the girl out of his head and he'd felt so ashamed that he just needed to get away.

The irony of it all did not escape him.

Self-loathing twisting his guts, he opened and closed his fist, working the feeling back into the stiff digits. They all moved. That was good, nothing broken, but they hurt pretty bad and the throbbing in the knuckles was enough to make him wince with each flex. Then again, that was good too. He deserved the pain.

Christ, I need a drink.

The thought came from out of nowhere but had a restorative effect that had Richard thumbing the shower panel. Pulling the curtain back before the deluge had ceased, he stepped out of the bath, grabbed a towel off the rail and, heedless of the water still running down his legs, made straight for the kitchen.

The oven's display showed it was just after two in the morning.

Out of habit, he made to fill the kettle, but then at the last minute opened the top cabinet. The British Empire might have been built on tea, but this called for something stronger. And he needed to get royally shit faced. Rummaging through the various jars, bottles, and tins, he retrieved the mostly full Bushmills they kept for when Alice's parents came to visit, before grabbing a glass from the draining board.

Pouring himself a measure, Richard threw his head back and downed the whiskey. It burned all the way down, but the liquor brought the warmth back, lessening the sickening knot rooted in his gut, so he savoured it all the same, relishing the hard flavour and distinctive aroma that curled up his nose-

"C-C-Christ," he bit out, coughing so violently each breath rasped like sandpaper, and his hand shook as he filled the glass again. This time making it a double, he stowed the bottle, and its now notably emptied contents, back into the cupboard before exiting the kitchen, drink in hand.

The living room had lost all its warmth as Richard half-sat, half-collapsed onto the sofa. Bathed in the soft light of the standing lamp they kept on a timer to dissuade thieves from getting ambitious, inky blackness pooled along the edges of the walls. Long shadows stretched across the floor like the bars of a cell. His cell.

Wary of another coughing fit that might rouse his wife, he only nursed the drink, sipping the dark amber liquid while staring over the rim of the glass at the dark outside the window.

What have I done?

Hardly a frequent or heavy drinker, the Bushmills made his eyes heavy and his head feel light as the alcohol took effect. The question haunted him, ringing through his ears while flashbacks of the last hour played out before his eyes.

His cock stiffened at the memory of Rebecca standing in the doorway in nothing but that robe. The way her slender curves rigged in his lap. The taste of her on his lips. Her breathy pleading as he tongued her clit. The feeling of her tight little cunt exploding around him...

He hated himself for what he'd done. He'd cheated on Alice, broken his vows to her and risked their marriage.

He'd used Rebecca, fucked her like a bitch in heat. Then, worse still, discarded her so callously even though he knew, well suspected, she had feelings for him.

God in fucking hell, he was a beast.

A part of him still couldn't believe it. Here in the safety of his home, on his sofa with a glass of whiskey, the night felt like a bad dream. A God damn fucking nightmare. Only he'd woken to it. The night was like a dream he could only half remember, slipping out of his grasp like pale wisps of morning mist curling around his fingers whenever he tried to focus on one moment. All except for those moments. They were sharp and clear and played before his eyes whenever he'd closed them.

What the fuck was wrong with him? He and Alice were finally getting their lives back to a sense of normality… How was he going to look her in the eye again, knowing that he'd… Christ, what would she say? What would she do? He'd ruined everything. And just when it had all seemed to be going so well. In layman's terms-

"I'm fucked." He toasted the declaration by downing the rest of his Bushmills. "Oh God. *Al*, I'm sor-"

The timer on the lamp's plug clicked over, cutting the power.

Darkness consumed him

Chapter One

There was comfort in sleep. The fool and coward's comfort. The comfort of hiding in the dark and fooling himself it had all been a dream.

Caught between sleeping and waking, Richard stared up at the ceiling. Autumn morning half-light crept through the curtains over the bed, turning their bedroom dark and grey. He didn't hear the cars speeding down Stroud Road, trying to beat the early morning rush hour, or the occasional gurgles coming through the baby monitor. Nor see the furniture taking shape in the gloom. He didn't want to wake up.

He wanted to sleep and dream and pretend. Better that than face reality and the consequences of what he'd done. Having to see his wife every day, holding her in his arms, making love to her, looking into her eyes, seeing the love there, and knowing, just knowing, he'd betrayed her.

Yes, he didn't want to wake, but the warm body wriggling beside him made it inevitable…

He blinked when a hand brushed up his side. Long, delicate fingers, feeling up his ribs and across his stomach. Then there was only softness and warmth. And a faint hint of cinnamon.

A sideways glance showed Alice sleeping next to him on a bed of her mahogany tresses. She must have rolled onto his side sometime in the night and, half covered by the quilt, was curling into him, head resting on his shoulder. She looked so peaceful. Content. Utterly oblivious to everything that had taken place through the night.

Her peace tore at him. Yet he was captivated and watched her sleep regardless, her delicate beauty enrapturing him the way the radiance of the moon enslaves a wolf.

He had to tell her, but how? A part of him wanted to confess now and have done with it. To wait would only make things harder, more complicated.

Excuses flitted through his mind. He was drunk. He'd been desperate. It hadn't meant anything. It was the usual line-up of dirt-bag husband excuses. Though he made sure to steer WELL clear of anything even hinting Alice bore some responsibility. That would not go down well.

Once, he even contemplated suggesting Rebecca had instigated it all. That got chucked out as quickly as it came. No matter what, he needed to keep the girl out of this.

As fond as she was of their babysitter, Richard knew his wife well enough to know she did not share her toys. And if that confrontation with Scarlet last night had just been Alice marking her territory...

Then, he had a pretty good idea of what she would do to him.

That thought made the idea of letting her sleep in a little longer, all the more tempting.

"Alice..." he mumbled. She'd think it odd if he didn't wake her. It would make her suspicious…

Alice mumbled something unintelligible in answer. Still more or less asleep, she shifted closer to nuzzle the hollow of his neck.

Richard stiffened at the contact, a shiver of pleasure rippling up his spine.

Her very closeness was an aphrodisiac. The feeling of her pressed against him, long willowy legs brushing over his calf, full breasts crushed against his side through her cropped sleeping sweater. And her mouth. God, that wicked mouth, brushing so softly over his skin, a mere tease of contact, igniting and sending tingling sensations surging through his skin down to the base of his spine.

Suddenly awake, alert, and very aware of that tale-tell stirring between his legs, Richard blinked, then glanced down to see blue-green eyes looking up at him.

For the longest moment, Alice only watched him, lips pursed and eyes bright with a look that had his cock suddenly harder than steel. Then, slowly, she pivoted, propping her head up enough to rest her chin on his ribs. "When did you get in?"

"Late." The vision of her had the words sticking to the back of his throat. "Did you wait long?"

She moaned a low throaty affirmative, placing a soft kiss just above his nipple while, in a tease of friction, one deliciously long leg slid across to straddle his thigh, making Richard all the more aware of the feeling of her body on his. And the dampness pushing against his leg. She was soaked. The silky heat of her arousal burned through her panties as she stretched out, caging him beneath her, as she walked soft butterfly kisses up his torso.

"I couldn't sleep," Alice purred, her words low and throaty without a trace of sleep. She bit down on his earlobe and tugged, fingers teasing down the flat of his stomach to his boxers. "I just kept thinking about you pushing me up against the fridge, grinding this big, hard cock into my pussy." Long fingers closed around him through the cotton of his underwear, holding, squeezing, then rubbing. "It got me so hot. In the end, I needed Antonio…"

Richard had to bite back a moan. Antonio was Alice's name for the B.O.B her friend Samantha had bought them as a gag gift for their 5-year anniversary. The image of his wife stretched out on their bed, her luscious body arching in throes of pleasure as she worked the toy between her legs, turned his cock to steel within her grasp. Until he recalled just what he had been doing while she had been putting on such an exquisite display and the knot of guilt that lodged inside his gut threatened to chase his erection away.

Alice's mouth claimed his, her tongue sweeping in with lush licks that sent tingles shivering up his spine and brought him back to full mast.

She took his mouth hungrily, her lips moving over his, full and soft and completely at odds with the hot demand that seemed at once to make his head spin while keeping his attention fixed solely on her. And all the while, she was stroking him. Slowly, her tiny hand unable to encompass his girth, but pumping him from root to tip in long, knowing motions, had him instinctively rocking into her, grinding his groin against her palm.

God, how did she always know? Know just how to touch him, how to play his body like a fiddle?

It was maddening. He needed to touch her, but no sooner had his fingers swept through the lush fall of silky locks to tease over her spine than she pulled back.

"I-it got me so horny," she panted, trailing hot little kisses down the line of his jaw. "Knowing you could barge in at any moment and catch me playing with Antonio. I wanted you to watch, to see what you did to me, see how wet I got thinking about your big dick," she spoke slowly, every low throaty syllable an intoxicating seduction. "I was right here, riding my B.O.B, waiting for you to come and see what a naughty wife you have. But you never came. Then I remembered you were up there with Rebecca. Is that why you left me all alone?" Her mouth was everywhere, kissing every bit of skin she could reach as she shuffled slowly back...

Her tongue dragged over his nipple, down the plane of his chest to the elastic of his shorts, only to pull away. "A-Alice..."

His wife rose slowly to sit straight backed between his legs, throwing the covers off, and pushing the lush fall of her hair back behind her ears, the pink of her tongue sliding across those full lips as her eyes found his. Then, "Was she a bad girl for you?"

Oh fuck!

"What?" Ice rushed down his spine and it was all Richard could do to keep the panic from his voice. Fuck, she knew. How could he have been so stupid? Of course, Alice knew. How could she not? Now he was-

"Was she a bad girl?" Alice said again, her voice seeming to grow even more playful as she leaned down to where his erection was visibly straining against the confines of his shorts, the slick tip pushing up from beneath the elastic to leave a slick and shiny trail around his belly button. "Was she still wearing that sexy outfit she had on last night? That cute little pink top and those faded jeans."

Warm air rushed over his crown as those full luscious lips wrapped around him through his underwear and slid up to bite the waistband and tug it back to reveal the fullness of his desire. "Or had she changed into something different, something special, for your eyes only? Stockings? High heels. Maybe a pink babydoll-mmm..." She licked him. The point of her tongue slid slowly up the centre of his column in a long drag from base to tip. "Did you like seeing her like that? Flaunting her body for you in a naughty nighty, her ass and legs on full display, those lush tits peeking out, begging to be sucked. And what about her pussy, that tight, juicy little pussy? Did she taste good?"

Mouth dry and desire shivering through him, Richard couldn't stop the words, "So-so goo-oohh!"

Lips stretched wide and checks hollowed, Alice took the head into her mouth and sucked him greedily. She took her time, going neither fast nor slow, but with all the determination of a woman who loved giving head and wasn't afraid to let the world know it.

In a dark corner of his brain, Richard knew he should be disgusted with himself. Alice thought they were playing. To her, this was just a game to spice up the mood. She had no way of knowing he had been balls deep inside their neighbour's daughter last night. And to top it all off, instead of confessing his sin, he was letting her give him one hell of a blow job. But he couldn't resist. It had been so long since he'd felt those luscious lips wrapped around his dick. And her eyes…

Fuck, Alice's eyes were incredible. Deep and stormy, they seemed to shift between grey and blue depending on her mood, and he could stare into them for an eternity and never look away. There were times she had brought him to the brink of cumming with just a look.

It was at once too intense, yet not enough, and Richard had to fist the sheets against the urge to grab, claw, and drive her mouth all the way down on his cock. The lush heat of her mouth glided along his shaft, never taking more than an inch or two in. And so slow. Damnit, how can she be so slow…

"A-Alice…"

She pulled off just as slowly, her eyes burning into his all the way. "Mmm-did you make her your new little cock whore? I bet she was just begging for this big dick." She fluttered her tongue over the slit, making his whole cock tingle and his butt clench. Then she was licking him, that little pink tongue sliding up and down his length. "Did you make her beg for your cock?"

He couldn't think or focus on anything but the feel of her tongue. Then she was taking him back into the delicious heat of her mouth, her head bobbing up and down, the delicious suction of those full lips sliding along his shaft, drawing him deeper. It was too much.

"Yes."

Alice moaned her approval, her eyes bright and burning into his as she pulled off. With one small hand still stroking him, she crawled on all fours up the length of his body, slowly, with her body low and back just that bit arched so he could feel the weight of her breasts dragging up his belly, soft and warm through her thin cotton cardigan, before she reared, like Aphrodite rising from her pool to straddle his waist.

"Oh, you're so bad," she purred, and gave him one final stroke before bringing her fingers up to her mouth and sucked them clean with a low moan. "Mmm… I can taste her on your cock. Did she drop to her knees and suck your big, yummy, married dick first? Or did you just bend her over and fuck her brains out?"

Jesus, her games were going to kill him. "N-neither, I-oh…"

The words trailed away in a low moan as she rolled her hips, sliding his cock along her folds through her soaked panties, showing him how wet she'd gotten. Then, with her right hand, she hooked two fingers beneath the garment and pulled it back, exposing her pussy to his gaze.

"Mmm… yeah baby, what did you do?" Alice purred, taking his cock in her left hand and coating his crown in her cream before pressing it hard against her clit with a slow roll-

She stilled, that sweet little mouth dropping in a voiceless gasp as Richard's hands seized her hips and held her fast as he began working his thick crest into her moist heat. "This."

He'd had enough.

Breath seething, Richard could barely contain himself as he pulled her to him. Even after all their years together, and the birth of their son, she was still so deliciously snug, and he could feel her plush walls stretch as he filled her inch by inch until she'd sheathed to the hilt. The perfect fit for his cock.

"Oh… Oh god! Baby wa-wait…" Alice gasped, her eyes unfocused. Reaching back, she grasped his knees to brace herself. "Not so… you're too… too-oh god!"

Breathless, Richard could only nod, her slight movement altering his angle of penetration. It wasn't much. Just enough to send a rush of sensation up his spine as her slick, velvety walls wrapped around his cock, pulsing and sucking him in as deep as he could go.

The prior night was gone and done. Now it was only them and he bit, chewed, and clawed against the instinctive urge to throw his wife on the bed and just take her. It had been weeks since the last time they'd gone a few rounds. She'd need time, time to adjust, time to get used to the feeling of being filled with him. So instead Richard just watched her, drinking in the sight of Alice straddling him, her head tipped back, the bounty of lush mahogany tresses cascading down to the small of her back, the plunging neckline of her cardigan revealing a feast of golden skin as her breasts strained against the cotton, imprisoned from his view by a few struggling buttons.

He wanted to see more. He wanted to see her.

"Mmm… you feel amazing, so tight," he purred, reaching up to tug the button from its fastening, bearing her full and luscious cleavage. "And such beautiful tits."

"Yeah, better than hers?" Alice panted, her back curling in offering as he sat up and took the peak of a single dusky nipple into his mouth.

"Much."

He teased her mercilessly, raining soft kisses down across her breasts, his wily tongue lashing down and around, refusing to pay her nipple any attention. Her skin was growing hot and he could feel her shake in his arms, pleading for more. Yet she held on until he sucked the stiff peak into his mouth, his hands crushing her to him and grinding her down on his cock with just the right amount of force to make her creamy walls pulse around him.

"Liar."

Low and breathy, the heat in her words sent a shiver straight down his spine, moments before long fingers fisted in hair and dragged his head back. Dark and lustful, Alice's eyes burned hungrily into his as she lowered her full lips to his, her lush tongue claiming him in a possessive dance that both thrilled and terrified him.

This wasn't part of her game. She wanted him to know he was hers. Her husband. Her lover. He was her man, no matter what, and he'd better not forget it.

She rolled her hips, breaking the kiss and rising until only half of him remained inside her.

"Mmm… Mr Martin," a soft, girlish voice purred. His heart leaping into his throat, Richard's eyes shot up to meet Rebecca's big doe eyes, his wife's sharp, angular face now soft and long. Then, she dropped back down, her lush heat clenching down, like a second mouth sucking him in…

Bolting upright, Richard just managed to brace himself on the armrests of his chair as it righted itself and almost pitched him headfirst into his desk. What the-

Reality caught up with him. He wasn't at home. He was at work in his office.

Sweating, heart pounding and his cock straining against his trousers, he collapsed back into the treacherous piece of furniture. Cupping his hands over his head and dragging his fingers down his face, he did his best to bite down on a sarcastic laugh. "Thank God. Just a dream-"

"Yo Dick, you feeling alright mate?"

Chapter Two

It never ceased to amaze Richard how, even when dressed to meet Holmes & Raine's business dress code, Mark McClaine always had the look of a second-hand car salesman. It was his perpetual grin. With that boot polish-black hair and moustache, it made him look like John Challis's Boycie in Only Fools and Horses, just without the sincerity.

Perched in the open door with his arms crossed, he was grinning at Richard like the cat that had got the cream. "Not looking too good there, Dick. Everything okay at home?"

"Yeah, I'm fine mate." Richard forced a smile. "Just, just got a lot on my mind, that's all."

Mark gave a dry laugh. Then, still grinning, he straightened and strolled over to his desk, the closest to the door, and dropped into his chair. He spun it around to face Richard in the adjoining cubicle. "I bet you do."

Richard did his best to ignore him. Him, and the chill that shivered down his spine. It wouldn't do any good. McClaine was like a Jack Russell with an old sock whenever he got the sense he was getting under someone's skin. And that was all he had, a scent, an inkling. Just a hunch. He didn't, couldn't know.

He was waiting for him to bite. Richard could see the mirth dancing in his eyes and knew it would be a mistake. So instead, he turned back to his computer. The screen was asleep, but a quick nudge of the mouse brought it alive. Prompted by a security box, he entered his password then watched the various excel spreadsheets pop back up. He bit back a groan. Would it have been too much to ask for a computer virus, or maybe just a good old power cut?

The Prometheus Account.

It had been due well over a week ago, and Scarlet had been on at him to get it done and on her desk by the end of the day.

He'd been working on it all morning, but with everything that had happened, his head just wasn't in the right place. And all the while, Mark had watched him, grinning that inane, shit-eating grin. Just the prospect of a long afternoon of it all over again had him blindly reaching out for his mug of tea. It was cold as ice, but he didn't care.

McClaine cocked a brow. "Ya know that tea's been sitting there all morning, right?"

"Mhm…" Richard murmured, chugging it down, not even tasting it as the memory of Rebecca purring his name in that hot wanton tone burned his ears.

Mr Martin…

"I flushed my pen out in it while you were in the land of nod."

"Mhh-" Eyes widening as the words and the acrid ink flavour registered, Richard pivoted and retched, spitting out the vile mixture into the waste bin beside the desk. "You… asshole!" Coughing, it took everything he had not to hurl the mug at McClaine. What little of his curse made it through the spluttering, however, was lost in the other man's laughing.

"Hey! Why aren't the pair of you out for lunch? Trying to bugger each other over the desk or something?"

Wiping his mouth with the back of his hand, Richard shot a withering sideways glance at Dave Sing. "Or something."

A third generation English-Nepalese, from the generation who had turned their back on the ancestral beliefs and completely assimilated to western culture, Dave Sing was also tall and thin. Handsome, with almond skin and copper eyes, but jet black that hair that he kept short and spiked. He'd joined the firm shortly after Richard, a fresh-faced graduate from Coventry University. Young and ambitious- Richard liked him well enough. An asset to the team, but in dire need of seasoning.

His own lunch in hand, the office's third resident settled in his own seat and was about to take a bite of a generous beef burger when he got his first close-up look at

Richard. The burger dropped into its wrapper. "Geez Rich, you look awful."

"Yeah-"

"Yeah, well, what do you expect?" McClaine cut in, just managing to get control of his guffaw. "Ben Dover here had a wild weekend after the do last week."

"What?" Richard rounded on him, his heart in his throat. No, he couldn't know about Rebecca. There was no way he could know, unless-

"Oh, come on, Dick, don't give us any of that old pony. That look your missus got when she saw old Walrus Face's daughter putting the moves on you. You can't honestly expect us to believe you didn't get a little bit. Alice damn near started fucking you right there in front of everyone."

"Fuck off," Richard warned, but inside he felt the knot his insides had wound loosen. Slightly.

McClaine shot Sing a sly look and added under his breath, as if to keep the man sitting just meters away from hearing, "Pity she didn't. What I wouldn't do to see that fine ass bouncing-"

"*Mike!* I'm warning you," Richard growled. "Shut your fucking hole or the next thing out of your mouth will be your teeth." He emphasised the threat by pushing back from the desk and rising to his feet, the rancour contorting his features into a look of such maleficence it had both Sing and McClaine backing away.

McClaine raised both hands in supplication, his face turning pale. "Woah, Dick, woah. I'm just busting your balls. Okay. Okay? I-I I'm sorry. Jeez… just relax. Relax." He was on his feet and backed round the desk.

Richard watched him go, letting him put a bit more space between them before dropping back into his chair.

All the tension seeming to evaporate from the room at once, and McClaine let go of a deep sigh. "We cool? God, my heart's beating so fast I think you were about to give me a coronary."

"Well, you do deserve it from time to time." Richard kept the bitterness from his tone. McClaine was the sort who needed a slap now and then, and he'd enjoyed the opportunity. No matter what, he loved his wife too much to let that sort of slander pass unchastised, but it wasn't worth settling at work. She'd be the first to tell him that. A man has to do what a man has to do, and the first thing a man had to do was to care for his family. Everything else, including giving mouthy gits a smack in the gob, came later.

"Ouch! That hurt. No, seriously mate, what's with you today? You've been bumbling around her like a zombie high off its head."

"Well, can you blame him?" Sing looked up, his burger already much reduced. "You said it yourself. Scarlet has it pretty wet for him. And you've heard the stories."

"Yeah, but come on, you don't believe all that shit, do you? What would she have to gain?"

"What do you mean, what would she have to gain?" Sing looked incredulous; his speech momentarily dissolved into the singsong accent of the Hindu.

"Why would Scarlet want to sleep with Tommy Cox or that asshole Mike in legal? She's a bird. They don't spread their legs for their underlings. What could they do for her? I mean, she's the big boss's daughter. Why should she shag anyone in the firm? If she wants a promotion, or a pony, all she has to do is ask 'Daddy', and Walrus Face will give his little princess anything she wants."

"Please, that is such misogynistic bullshit. A woman can be every bit as abusive as a man. Haven't you read Disclosure?"

"I saw the film," McClaine cut in, and then his features twisted with a leer. "And I tell you, that Demi Moore can suck my cock any day…"

Richard was only half listening to them. He had heard the stories, too. And like McClaine, usually dismissed them as idle office gossip.

Whatever else she might be, Scarlet was undoubtedly a very beautiful woman, and beautiful women in positions of power and authority attracted rumours the way a dog drew fleas. Often as not, they were just stories spread by jealous colleagues or bitter subordinates left in her wake- and Scarlet wasn't short of those. Quite the reverse in fact, but she was also the daughter of the firm's MD, Derick Holmes. The consequence for any employee caught besmirching her good name would be unpleasant, but after their encounter on Friday, Richard was no longer entirely convinced all the stories were *just* stories, but he wasn't about to admit it.

There'd been a look in her eyes. A certain, predatory gleam...

"Okay, that's enough," Richard snapped. "Have either of you actually spoken to anyone who actually fucked her? Or heard a story that wasn't from a guy who spoke to a guy?"

McClaine's grin dropped. "No."

"Well no," Sing admitted, shoving the empty burger box into a desk drawer. "But Jasper Hawkins told me he once saw her going down on the girl from the mailroom." He looked vindicated.

Until McClaine asked, "Umm, Davey-boy, remind me, what happened to Jasper Hawkins?"

Sing shrugged. "Walrus Face kicked him to the curb."

"For?"

"Improper conduct."

Rich barked a triumphant laugh. "Ha! Exactly, telling tales about his daughter. See, he was talking out of his arse and got canned for it. So, with that cleared up, can we get off this subject? I don't fancy getting sued for libel."

"Slander," Sing corrected.

"What?"

"Libel's written. You mean you don't fancy getting sued for slander."

Richard gave him the finger. "Oh, shut it Apu. I don't give a damn. If you have to be so pedantic, why don't you take a look at this," he scouted back, making room for the pair. Sing and McClaine exchanged a look, then pushed back from their own desks and walked around to his. "I told Scarlet I'd get this report over to her this morning, but the numbers don't add up. I don't know. Is there something I'm not seeing?"

"So?" McClaine asked, coming up to peer over Richard's shoulder. "You know the drill. If it doesn't add up, just attach an advisory."

Sing nodded in agreement. "That's company policy."

Hemmed in by the tight confines of the one-person cubicle, Richard felt the room growing noticeably stuffier. "I know, but something just doesn't feel right."

"Geez, Dick!" McClaine exclaimed, slapping a hand down on the desk. "Why are you making this so hard for yourself? You know the bitch has a major stick up her ass about this sort of thing. Just give her the report. It's not your job anymore-"

"Mr Martin?"

The semi that had been slowly diminishing surged to renewed life as Richard's heart leapt into his throat, his head snapping up. And then he was back there in that bedroom, naked, with *her* stretched out beneath him, his cock buried to the root in her lush, grasping heat. That sweet voice hot and panting in his ear.

"Ah… ahhh-oh my God-oh my God-oh my God… I can't take it… it's too much… too big!" she shrieked, her fingers clawing at the walls and eyes wide with pure ecstasy. "Oh yes… yes… don't stop… I'm all yours Mr Martin… I've wanted your hard cock inside me for so long… you can fuck me whenever you want to… just don't stop… don't stop!"

Rebecca stood in the office doorway.

It was the first he'd seen of the girl since their tryst Friday night, and she looked amazing.

Her white button up blouse was smart and conservative, and while too short to reach her knees, that skirt would have to go a hell of a lot higher to offend any granny's delicate sense of decency, or workplace dress code. Yes, there was nothing overtly sexual in her attire, but the thought of what she hid underneath- those lush full tits, her tight athletic build, made it all sexy as hell. And she was gorgeous, too. Her dark chestnut hair had been tied into its customary side braid and there was a little dusting of blusher to her checks, but it was her lips that caught his eyes first. There was a glossiness to them that immediately made him ache to kiss her, taste her…

She must have come straight from work; it was the only time she wore make-up.

"Hi Rebecca." The words sounded feeble, but it was the best he could do on the spot. Though he'd known this moment would eventually come, he'd been so obsessed with what he'd tell Alice, he'd never actually thought about what to say to Rebecca. "What are you doing here?"

"Mrs Martin called. She thought you might be getting hungry." She beamed a sweet girlish smile and held up a plastic bag. "You forgot your lunch."

"Ah… Thanks… Rebecca," he nodded, feeling suddenly embarrassed. He'd been in such a fluster that morning he'd left his Tesco's pasta salad in the fridge and hadn't noticed until he'd been halfway to work. "Just plonk it down over on that cabinet other there. I'll get to it in a bit. How much do I owe you?"

She beamed, sweeping past him and around the desks. "Don't sweat it, it's on me."

"Really?" He pivoted in his chair to follow her. "You sure about that?"

"Yeah, it's nothing. I wanted to check out the Victorian Market anyway, so it's no big deal." Her smile seemed to broaden. "And I got a *big* bonus over the weekend."

A big bonus? Fuck, what did she mean? Richard felt cold fingers trail down his spine. Was she planning to blackmail him, to keep what happened a secret? He wouldn't have thought so. The girl generally had all the sly cunning of a Care Bear. Then again, she had told Alice, and who had secretly told him, that she'd been saving to move out and get away from her father.

Hush-money could go a long way there.

Or was she after something else?

Something more *physical*.

The prospect made the knot in Richard's gut tighten and he was torn between terror and being a little turned on. "That's cool. Well, thanks Rebecca. I owe you-"

"Urh, Mr Martin, could I have a word with you? Um..."

"Ah, well, now isn't really the best time. You caught us at a bit of a bad moment and-"

"Aw, don't be silly Dick, we can spare the girl a moment," McClaine's eyes glittered darkly as he gave the girl a slow, less than subtle once over.

Rebecca quickly twisted away from his scrutiny. "Er- no! No, I understand." Then she gave Richard a sideways glance, a small smile curling those lush pink lips. "If you want, you could just pop round later... If you have the time that-that is, that is, please, I don't want to put you out and my dad will be out so -"

"Ah... No, that's alright." Remembering her standing at the door in that little black *thing*, Richard swallowed. He couldn't be alone with her, not there. He was safe here. This was his work; she wouldn't try anything here.

And more importantly, nor would he.

He glanced nervously at his co-workers. They were both grinning like a pair of mangy hyenas. "Mind giving us a minute, lads?"

"Sure." McClaine gave Sing a nudge. "Come on Apu, let us leave Dick Hefner here to tend to his little lady friend." However, he paused by the door after the smaller man had gone through and threw a sideways glance back at Richard. "Oh, and enjoy yourself Dick, you're more in need of a blow job than any other white man in history."

Bastard.

Richard cursed and turned away, flipping him the V-Sign over his shoulder. It was an almost impotent retort, but it was the best he could do with Rebecca in such close proximity. He couldn't risk over reacting. He couldn't take the chance of giving his work mate cause to think something was going on.

So he kept his attention locked on his screen, even after the door shut and the laughter drowned out by the hum of computer drives. Yet his eyes had a mind of their own and every few moments he caught himself glancing over in her direction as Rebecca jumped up to perch her ripe little derriere on the edge of his desk, her pencil skirt riding up as she crossed her legs to flash him a hint of thigh.

Thighs that had been wrapped around him just days ago.

Growing ever more aware of the stiffness between his legs, while his guts twisted into knots, Richard swivelled around to face her, blindly tapping a few keys to minimise the spreadsheets. Not that he thought she would have any interest in them, but PPI was such a hot topic, better safe than sorry.

Forcing down a dry swallow, he smiled pleasantly at her. "So, what's so urgent?"

"Well… I wanted to… um it's just that… Well…" She looked away, a blush staining her cheeks a dusty pink. "I'm sorry. About what happened on Friday, I don't know what got into me…"

"I think I have some idea." He couldn't help a dry chuckle.

"I didn't mean like that," Rebecca laughed, the sound high and girlish, breaking the tension that had been building between them.

For a moment.

Then the dam broke, and she started to cry. Fat, glassy tears rolled down her checks in rivers. "I'm so sorry, Mr Martin. I didn't mean for it to happen. Please, please don't hate me. I- I couldn't…"

Her tears raked him. "Hey, hey, hey, come here." Richard opened his arms. She all but threw herself at him, burying her face into his neck and sobbing loudly as he hugged her back. "It's okay, sweetheart. It wasn't your fault. Everything just happened so fast…"

Not sure what else to do, he held her till the tears passed, and then he continued to hold her, rocking gently from side to side. It felt good to hold her like this. She felt good. Her hair was silky soft against his cheek. That lean athlete's build fitting against him so perfectly, warm and so very inviting. Those lush young breasts pushing against his chest through the material of her uniform, tipped by dusky nipples that just begged to be sucked.

"Mr Martin?" Rebecca voiced, her tone shaky and uncertain, and he was suddenly aware she was looking down. Down at where the bulge was pitching a tent in his trousers.

Oh shit…

Heat burned across his cheeks as her head tilted back up to his, those full lips curling into a sly feline smirk.

"H-how was the market?"

No sooner had the words left his mouth, he knew they were a mistake.

Only, he had no idea what else to say. The question was the first thing that came to mind that didn't also involve the words fuck, cunt, cock, tits or cum- in one insidious combination or another.

"Oh… It's amazing!" She positively beamed at the question, her big doe eyes lighting up with mischief. "There are so many stalls this year, and the costumes. It's just like something out of Dickens' times."

"That's… nice. Err Rebecca I have to-"

She carried on regardless. "They've even set up a snow machine over the ice rink…"

"Rebecca-"

"But it's broken and…"

"Rebecca… look… I… I don't think-"

"You should hurry up and eat your sandwich, Mr Martin, before it gets cold."

"Rebecca…" He really needed her to stop talking.

"Mmm… it's pulled pork. I had the hog roast sausage. I normally prefer chicken, but when I saw them on the spit, I couldn't resist. They were just so big and thick; I wasn't even sure I could get it in my mouth-"

He took her mouth, kissing her hard and hungrily, drinking in her lushness.

It was madness. Utter madness. But Richard couldn't take it. He had to have her again. Pulling her into his lap, his hands slid down the lines of her narrow waist to cup and squeeze her butt through her skirt, crushing her to him, making her moan and arch. Fuck, she tasted even better than he remembered. There was no trace of cherries now. Only the lushness of her soft pink lips, and she was all the sweeter for it.

Rebecca didn't waste a moment. Burying her hands in his hair, she sucked his tongue like a woman possessed and moaned a low purr that vibrated through him and made his trapped cock throb against its confines.

Yet it wasn't enough. Nowhere near enough. He wanted more. He wanted her, wanted to rip her shirt open and taste those plump tits. Wanted to bury his face between her legs and eat her hot, wet cunt. Wanted to bend her over his desk, go balls deep in that tempting little pussy and fuck her like the hot little bitch she was.

She moaned a pitiful protest when he left her mouth, but it quickly turned to small kittenish gasps as he nipped a fiery trail down the long slope of her neck. Then she was like putty in his hands. Her hands dropped down to push his jacket halfway down his arms, before working on his shirt buttons, fumbling a bit as he sucked the sweet spot where her neck and shoulder met.

"Oh… Mr Martin!" Rebecca moaned, her head rolling back, exposing more skin for him to kiss. He greedily obliged, dragging the flat of his tongue along the dips and hollows of her throat. Meanwhile, his hands ground her on the ridge of his cock, sliding under the hem of her skirt and up to the warmth beneath. Up along the smooth, silky-soft skin of her inner thigh. Fingers stretching, brushing over taught tendons and reaching for the heat of her lush wet-

A door slammed shut somewhere down the hall, and Richard's heart leaped into his throat. He froze, a moment of clarity rushing over him in an icy cascade.

Shit!

"Stop. Stop- shh!" Seizing Rebecca's arms, he pushed her away, quite literally holding her at an arm's length as he threw a sideways look towards the door.

It was still shut, but the window would have given anyone passing by a front-row seat of their own dirty little peep show.

He watched it, not daring to blink.

Ten seconds.

Thirty seconds.

One minute and still nothing.

He let out a breath. That was close. He didn't want to think what might have happened if someone had seen them. Even now, with their flushed faces and dishevelled condition, it wouldn't have taken Doctor-bleeding-Spock to work out what had been going on.

"Mr Martin?"

Rebecca's voice was so quiet and unsure, it was almost a stranger's voice. He twisted back to face her, and the look in her eyes raked his soul. She couldn't have looked more hurt if he had slapped her.

"Rebecca…" The words caught in his throat. He'd seriously fucked up. Again. "We can't do this."

"Why not?"

Richard felt like the lowest piece of shit that had ever walked the earth. "You know why. I'm married, and I love my wife."

"She doesn't have to know."

"That's not the point. Alice deserves better than that, and so do you." Unable to look her in the eyes, he shrugged his jacket back into place before fixing his buttons. "I don't want to use you like that, Rebecca."

"I don't care. You can use me however you want. I-"

The sudden shrill shriek of a phone ringing cut her off. His computer monitor burst into life, and Alice's face stared back at them.

Chapter Three

"Get down," Richard snapped, not exactly pushing the girl away but urging her off of his lap and down under the desk with an insistence that brokered no argument from her. Then, heart pounding like a drum in his chest, he turned back to the screen.

The Skype video call was getting close to timing out.

Resisting the urge to glance down to the girl's hideaway, he accepted the video call, then forced a broad smile. "Hey Al."

His wife's avatar minimised, and Alice's smoky gaze met his.

"Not interrupting anything, am I, *Dick?*" Even wrapped around an insinuation, her husky tone made his dick hard all over again.

Or maybe it was just the sight of her all dressed up in her '*work wear*'. No doubt, the sight of Alice in that tan blazer, button up blouse, and white pencil skirt had fuelled more than a few teenage boys to lock themselves in the toilets for an extended break.

"Nah, just taking my break. How's work?"

"Boring," she pouted. "I seem to spend all day either marking half-term homework or giving out detentions... Errr, I hate November."

"Aww... don't worry, love, it'll soon be Christmas."

She rolled her eyes. "Ha... ha... ha... Don't remind me."

Alice loved her work. She loved being a teacher, but there were times when the job didn't love her. "Speaking of Christmas, you left your lunch at home, so I gave Rebecca a call and asked her to pop in with something special for you."

Her tone was playful, but the edge to her voice sent a shiver down his spine, and he found himself glancing down at the dark space under his desk.

"Yeah... she just left." He picked up his still wrapped sandwich and held it up for her to see.

A ghost of a smile curved the corner of her mouth and the tip of her tongue darted out across her plump upper lip. "Mmm... good, because I have a little surprise for you."

Momentarily lost in all the memories of just what that tongue and mouth could do, Richard could only swallow. "Oh..."

She leaned back in her big black chair and began working on the buttons of her blouse. "I admit I was rather miffed with you over the weekend for getting in so late the other night, but I think I know a way for you to make it up to me..."

Richard couldn't believe his eyes. "Jesus, Alice... are you mad?"

"Come on *Dick*, I don't have long till my next class... mmm... one of my students might come by at any minute..." As the last button came undone, the blouse fell open to tease him with a glimpse of her breasts, full and firm and absolutely luscious, before she pressed it closed. "Whoopsie..."

"Tease."

"Aww... remember how we used to do this whenever one of us was working late... come on baby..." She let one corner of the garment slide down to reveal her left breast before cupping it. "Mmm... you like these baby, God I wish you were here... I'm so horny... I just want to jerk your big dick off with my tits and watch you paint them with all your yummy cum..."

Richard had to force himself to breathe as he watched his wife raise her tit up to her mouth and swirl her tongue around the pebbled nipple. She knew how much he loved her tits. Knew just how to use them to drive him wild.

"A-Alice..."

"Do you want me to beg for it... want me to get down on my hands and knees... and beg to see your cock..." The blouse fell open completely as Alice pushed her breasts together, making them bounce and jiggle before rolling the dusky nipples between her fingers and thumbs. "Mmm… you're so bad. Do it, Dick, I want your cock."

And his cock definitely wanted her.

That throaty husk of hers had him as hard as steel.

Sensation rippled up and down his length as it fought to be free of its restraints. So insistent and demanding, his white knuckled grip on the armrests of his chair was all that kept him from ripping open his chinos and giving her the show she craved.

Then he felt something brush against his leg.

He froze.

He knew he shouldn't look, but his eyes had a will of their own. Drawn down like magnets to watch the slow seduction of a hand rising from under the desk. Slowly, step by step, walking up his leg bit by bit towards the bulge of his cock, getting closer and closer and…

"*Fuck*…" A ragged breath left him in a rush as soft digits curled around his imprisoned length and gave it a testing squeeze.

"That's it, grab it baby, tell me how big it is… so big and hard and full of cum…" Alice panted in her hot breathy tone, the fingers of her left hand roughly attending to her nipple, twisting and tugging in the way that always got her hot. "Just thinking about you sitting there, jerking your big dick for me… mmm… gets me so wet. Does it feel good, Dick?"

"Yeah… so fucking good…" Richard groaned, Rebecca's small hand fisting him through his trousers, pumping along his length from root to head, her movements slow but urgent. He tried to focus on the screen, on his wife, to blot out the sensations Rebecca was sending sizzling through him, but he was too finitely aware of her. Aware of her shuffling closer, her head of dark chocolate hair creeping out from beneath the table, her free hand creeping up his other leg. Moving higher and higher towards his zipper.

He needed to stop this. He needed to stop her, but when he tried, his body had a will of its own. Instead of pushing her away, his hands just undid the fastenings of his belt and trousers. Then Rebecca's hand was dragging him from the confines of his boxers, and it was too late.

"Suck it." The command was out before he knew what he was saying.

"Fuck yes, baby, I love sucking your cock…" Alice moaned on the screen, thinking the command was for her. "I really wish you were here. Your cock's so big and tasty. I could suck it all day, jerking you off with my tits until you paint my face with your cum. Or would you just bend me over and pound-pound me… pound me from behind…"

She was getting close; he could hear it in her voice. Richard could imagine her hand under the desk, fingers pushing under the silk of her panties to rub her clit. "Stick it in me Dick. I need it. I've been such a naughty schoolgirl, bend me over your desk and punish me… punish me with it… spank my ass with your cock and use my naughty little pussy… she's so nice and hot and wet for you… just begging to get your dick off- oh shit!"

Through the speakers, the school bell sounded faint and distant, but it hit Alice like ice.

In a flash, she was up and pulling herself together as the hall outside filled with the shouts and bangs of children running to their next class. "Sorry babe, gotta go, but we'll finish this later," she promised, before killing the Skype connection with a click of her mouse.

Richard hardly noticed.

Instead, his eyes never strayed from the vision of Rebecca's big doe eyes staring up at him from beneath her bangs as her pink lips wrapped around his cock. A picture of innocence and wickedness. Then she was taking him in. Those lush lips brushing over his glands and down his shaft. The wet heat of her mouth enveloped him, sucking him in all the way to the gate of her throat, before pulling back to mouth his sensitive crown.

"You've no idea how long I've wanted to do this, Mr Martin," she purred, teasing his underside with slow licks. "I'm sorry, I know it's wrong, but after Friday night, I just can't help myself…"

"It's okay Rebecca, that wasn't… it-it's not your fault."

Richard groaned, his head rolling back as the hand still holding him began pumping up and down.

"It's alright, Mr Martin. I know you're only saying that. It's all my fault. I'm such a naughty girl, going down on you while you're talking to your wife. Have I been bad, Mr Martin?"

"Yeah, so very bad."

"Do you like it Mr Martin?

"*Yes*." The feeling was so intense that Richard's death grip almost snapped the arms clean off his chair.

"Are you going to punish me?"

"Oh yes, I'm going to put you over my knee alright, and if you don't make me cum quickly, I'll bend you over and fuck you across this desk until you can't walk straight."

"Oh, promises, promises…"

She took him back into her mouth. Her cheeks hollowed as she sucked hard, head bobbing up and down while fisting his root, making up whatever she lacked in experience with enthusiasm.

"Mmm… yes, yes, yes… just like that…" Richard groaned, almost as much for her benefit as for his, the words just tumbling out as he melted back into his chair. His hands lost themselves in the silky softness of her hair. He gathered up and pushed back a wing of dark chocolate that had fallen out of place, before fisting it as the flat of her tongue swirled around his crest once, twice, thri- *oh fuck!*

The sensation came upon him so quickly, he didn't have a chance to voice a warning before his hot cum fired into her greedy mouth. His orgasm ripped through him hard enough for black spots to dance before his eyes, but Rebecca accepted everything he had to give her.

She drank every drop. Swallowing greedily as it flowed, sucking when the tide ebbed. And all the while watching him, those big doe eyes bright with… what?

Satisfaction at having brought him to orgasm so easily?

Or excitement about future possibilities?

Only when she had finally milked him dry and his fingers slipped from her hair did she release his still firm erection and stand back up. Taking the napkin from her uneaten sandwich, she wiped her lovely rosy lips clean.

Stepping around his chair, she lent down and pressed a soft kiss to his cheek.

"I better get back. See you later, Mr Martin."

"Rebecca wait-" Richard started, but her cute little derriere was already sashaying out the office, the door slamming shut behind her.

His fist hit the desk, hard enough to make the structure tremble. "Shit!"

You stupid bloody bastard, he cursed inwardly as guilt and shame raked him with claws of ice and fire, respawning the sicking knot deep in his guts. How the fuck could he have been so stupid to of let that happen, again?

A ping sounded from the computer, making Richard's heart leap into his throat. His head snapped up to see the icon for the unfinished report flash. The ping was a pre-programed reminder to warn the user whenever a file had been open and inactive for too long.

Richard contemplated it for a second. "Fuck it!"

Tapping a few keys, he deleted his notes, closed the document and forwarded it in an email to Scarlet's inbox.

They were right. It wasn't his job anymore. What the fuck did it matter, anyway?

Shoving himself into his trousers and refastening his belt, he grabbed his untouched sandwich and took a bite.

Only, he'd lost his appetite.

Chapter Four

"We're heading off, Dick. Catch you later."

Richard looked up from his monitor just in time to glimpse McClaine and Sing trot out the office with backhanded waves, like schoolboys ditching detention. "You guys off already?"

"*Already?* Do me a favour, Dick, take a day off, will ya."

"Go see the girls at Spearmint Rhino. They do your sort of favours, mate, not me."

McClaine shot him a look that could curdle custard, then raised his hand, pulled back his cuff and pointed to his TAG Heuer watch face. "See this? It's past five. That's clocking off time in my book. You might be prepared to work yourself ragged, but I've got better things to do than kill myself for old Walrus Face and little miss Tight Ass. Some of us have a life, ya know, see ya."

"You live with your mother!" Resisting the urge to flip him the finger, Richard turned back to his desk, his eyes landing on a mountain of paperwork. Work he'd been putting off while obsessing over the Prometheus Account.

He checked his own wristwatch, a Seiko his old man had given him for his eighteenth birthday. Sure enough, it was five thirteen in the afternoon. He'd been at it for five hours, five bloody hours, and hadn't even made a dent.

Bugger.

Exhaling a long, suddenly exhausted breath, he reclined back in his seat and pushed a hand through his hair. He supposed he should follow their lead and go home. This work could wait a night, and Alice would be on her way home soon enough, after she'd picked up Alex from her parents and battled her way up the stretch of M5 that connected Bristol and Gloucester, through the last of the rush hour traffic. They'd have a nice family dinner before sitting down to… what? Talk about their day?

That's good darling. My day? It was ok. I struggled a bit with that report, but Rebecca gave me a blowjob when she popped by. So all in all…

The thought had a dry laugh billowing up his throat.

How could he look Alice in the eyes again? Hold their son again?

No, he couldn't. Not now, not after…

The computer emitted a small double ring and an email notification window popped up in the bottom right-hand corner of the screen. It was from Scarlet, though the address attached read *Tight_Ass_Bitch.*

Officially, no one knew who had hacked her email to change the address. Whoever it was though, their joke had backfired. Far from being annoyed or embarrassed by the stunt, Scarlet practically adopted the title, and never missed an opportunity to live up to it.

True to her unofficial title, the message was brief and to the point.

> *Dick*
> *Drop by my office on your way out.*
> *We need to discuss Prometheus.*
> *Scarlet*

"… Shit," Richard cursed and looked mournfully back to the paperwork and the potential overtime it offered. "Well, that puts the kibosh on that plan."

He closed the mail with a click of his mouse.

The door was sleek pine with a bronze plaque embossed with the legend, **S. Holmes, Accounts Supervisor**.

Being the boss's daughter certainly had its perks.

Richard knocked once, then pushed on through without waiting for an answer.

Seated at the immense leather-topped oak desk that dwarfed her and the rest of the office, Scarlet was working on her laptop. Behind her, floor to ceiling windows boasted a picturesque landscape of the river below.

To a stranger, she might have looked oblivious, blind to the goings on around her, her focus dominated by her work, but Richard knew better. Scarlet was anything but oblivious. She was the sort of woman who woke up intending to conquer the world. Who missed nothing.

Without waiting for an invitation, he crossed the wood panelled floor, bypassing the plush leather sofa to take the simple leather and teak chair opposite her side of the desk.

She didn't look up, nod, or do anything to acknowledge his presence.

Nor would she. Not yet. Not until she was ready.

It was her game, a power play to remind the minion just who was the boss.

Well, at least she didn't make him pass her tea or pick pens off of the floor.

The office had been the department's briefing room before her appointment. Her predecessor had made do with the windowless coat cupboard three doors down. It was simple and functional, but large enough to impress. And beige. Very beige. Beige walls. Beige rugs. Beige leather…

Beige. Safe and soothing, and not at all Scarlet Holmes.

She was as bloody crimson as her namesake. And then a dash extra.

All heat and passion and searing raw emotion. And beauty.

Scarlet flaunted flawless skin, tanned to a soft peach hue, that complimented the waves of spun gold that tumbled down to her shoulders. She wore a tight white dress that showed off plenty of leg and had a deep plunging neckline to emphasise her figure. There wasn't a man alive who could deny Scarlet was *very* lovely.

The matter wasn't up for discussion. It was a fact.

And only skin deep.

Beneath the fragile beauty, she was as hard and sharp as steel. A lioness disguised in a little bunny's fur.

He ignored the urge to check his watch. That subtle hint would only prolong the game, though. Scarlet would see to that, sure enough. So instead, he amused himself by watching the goings on outside the tall windows behind her desk that overlooked the line of narrow boats and yachts moored along the Sharpness Canal.

The view was wasted on Scarlet.

When she turned to him, the bunny beamed up at him. "Hey Dick."

"Hi Scarlet," Richard smiled back, inwardly steeling himself. If she wanted to play her games, he'd play. "How was your day?"

It was a poor effort, but the best he could do on the fly. It got the job done.

"Oh, the usual, same shit, different day. You headin' home for the day?"

"Yeah soon, just had a couple of things I wanted to finish up first."

She ignored the prompt and just kept smiling up at him.

Sod it, she could have this round. "So, you wanted to see me?"

Her eyes were bright, and they laughed at him behind her glasses. She didn't need them. The lenses were from a cheap pair of reading glasses she'd got in a Pound shop, but the frames were designer and worth more than he made in a month. "Yes, we need to discuss Prometheus."

"Oh? How come?"

"Don't play coy with me, Dick." Despite her smile, behind the cheap plastic lenses, her eyes flared with blue fire. Behind the bunny, the lion was baring its fangs, a warning before the charge. "I told you I wanted you to make the Prometheus Account your top priority, yes?"

"Yes."

"Yes? That was a month ago. The report should have taken you a few days, max. And now you send me this?" She pulled a manilla folder out of a drawer and laid it open on the desk. A quick glance confirmed it was the paperwork he'd sent her earlier. "So, what's the game?"

"Game?"

"You could have knocked this up in a few hours. You have been, all afternoon. So, either you had a hunch, then lost your nerve, or you were slacking off to make me look bad. Which is it?" Closing the folder, she slid it aside, then leaned forward to face him, fingers tipped by perfectly manicured nails painted speckled gold, steepled under her chin.

"Scarlett I…"

"Do you have a problem working under me, Dick?"

"No."

"Then you had a hunch?"

"It was a stupid idea, not worth mentioning."

"You thought it was important enough to risk the contract."

Reaching into his pocket, he pulled out the flash drive with all his research into Prometheus and laid it on the desk. He'd forgotten about it amongst everything else that had gone on in the last couple of days and had only thought of it after receiving her email. He'd brought it along just in case. "It's nothing."

"Why don't you let me be the judge of that." She took the flash drive and plugged it into her desktop. With a few clicks of her mouse, all the documents were arranged on her monitor. Spreadsheets. Invoices. Tax returns. Everything he could find on Prometheus, but would it be enough?

A tight knot of tension wound around and around his guts like a python's coils. Financial reports. Richard watched her work. Those fierce blue eyes skimmed over the screen behind her glasses, moving from one article to the next while she caught her rose-pink lower lip between a perfect set of pearly whites.

He hated to admit it, but her look was sexy as hell.

She swivelled slowly back around in her chair to face him; her stare piercing. Not quite a lioness, but definitely not a flopsy bunny either. "All this shows is Prometheus recorded substantial profits. Hardy conclusive, *Dick*."

A low shiver coursed down his spine to tingle in his crotch as his cock stirred at the way she said his growingly official nickname. The accusation behind it made him feel like he was getting a telling off from the hot teacher all the boys fantasised about.

"Since the early 90s, Prometheus has consistently recorded growing profits. Yes, however, if you look more closely, you'll see the bulk of their earnings came from work throughout Ukraine, Estonia, Georgia, Kazakhstan, and the Baltic states. Nations recovering from the Soviet Union. Plenty of cheap labour, but a brassic economy. Prometheus's books took a slight hit in the Global recession but remained firmly in the black until 2012, when they expanded their operations into the Middle East. Work in areas of Turkey and Syria achieved record profits, despite the numerous conflicts raging in the region." He paused, trying to think how to put the next part.

"Go on…"

He took a breath, steeling his nerves for the plunge. "I think Prometheus has connections with Russian organised crime and is a front for criminal activity, including money laundering, drug trafficking and smuggling."

And there it was, the complete ruin of his career. And all packed up neatly in one sentence. Who says experience counts for nothing!

For the longest moment, Scarlet let the silence drag on. Her expression impassive, unreadable, neither bunny nor lion, but her eyes, once such a vibrant blue, were suddenly steel. "I see." Her tone was as cold and sharp as ice. "Those are very serious accusations, Dick. Ones we're required by law to report to the proper authorities and would almost certainly result in us losing the client, even if you're wrong. Can you prove this?"

"No," he confessed, then added hastily. "But there are too many anomalies for it all to be just coincidence."

"What anomalies?"

"The company was founded in the early 90s and received heavy outside funding, primarily from a now disbanded Russian-led consortium, at the same time Russian gangsters started moving west out of Moscow. They do business all over Europe but are especially affluent in areas of high Russian criminal activity and interest."

Scarlet nodded. "And their 2012 expansion?"

"The date they began expanding was just a month after the Russian President's second inauguration. It's not exactly a secret he uses the crime bosses as off the book enforcers, and the countries Prometheus has expanded to have seen heavy Russian influence since."

"They're war zones, Dick," she laughed without mirth, shaking her head. "Builders and developers often receive government contracts to repair and rebuild sites damaged in conflict."

"Yes, but usually after the war is won," Richard cut in. "I've heard of prudent planning, but if I'm wrong, whoever picked these deals must have one hell of a crystal ball. You should take him to the Cheltenham races next year. With this guy's luck, you'll make a fortune betting on the gee-gees."

She ignored the joke, instead turning back to look over the documents on her screen. "Well, the money laundering is self-explanatory. Dirty money finances the projects on the books, then returns as profits, but what about this trafficking and smuggling nonsense?"

What? Was she actually buying this story? He couldn't believe it; he'd half expected her to tear up his contract right there, even for suggesting it.

"They ship out their own equipment instead of hiring or purchasing on-site. A JCB is a pretty big bit of kit. Lots of places to hide something you don't want found, if you know how."

"But you can't prove it. Legally."

"No." His throat was so tight, he had to force the word out. "After tax is accounted for, their profits are all funnelled into an account in a private Depository Bank in Zurich. I can't track it from there without going through a long and costly legal battle."

"So…" she rounded on him, her voice as cold and sharp as steel. "Let me get this straight, because I'm a little confused. You're given a high value contract, told to make them your top priority, but instead of doing your job and having the report on my desk like you're supposed to, you dig into their business records and concoct some cock and bull theory about the Russian Mafia. And just to put the icing on the cake, you have no proof? Nothing to back it up. Is that about the sum of it?"

"More or less."

She sighed and shook her head.

That was it. She'd just fired her broadside and hit dead centre. He was sunk. He might as well go back and clear out his desk. Save the trip in tomorrow and have a lie in-

"Why did you keep digging? Why not just hand it in when you were supposed to after hitting a dead end?"

Richard had to work hard to keep his confusion from showing.

Why had he kept digging? Force of habit? Professional curiosity? His last job had done checks all the time, and he'd never let it go on for so long. There had just been something. Something not right. Something he couldn't put his finger on. Just something. Just…

"Just a hunch."

"A hunch?" She leaned back in her chair. "Well Dick, I don't know what to say, except…" Her full red lips spread into a wide smile, with just the hint of a white lion's fang. "Congratulations."

Chapter Five

Richard blinked, almost at a loss for words. Almost.

Congratulations? For what? Dropping a bollock? Making a complete ass of himself? "What?"

Scarlet's head titled, her eyes dancing and gleeful, both bunny and lioness. "Congratulations. You passed the test."

"Test? What test?" he demanded, incredulous.

"For the position of Financial Analyst," she said simply. "You applied for the position before being assigned to this department."

"Yeah, I remember."

How could he not?

It had been one of the few jobs he'd actually wanted. Similar seniority to his old role, but with a better salary and abundant career opportunities.

Or so the ad in the job centre had led him to believe.

What they'd offered was a polite brush off, followed by a role that was a major move down, with less pay, more hours and with every opportunity he could ever have hoped for, to kiss ass and get his ass kicked. However, with little Alex on the way, what choice had he had? It wasn't like he was getting headhunted by the Bank of England, after all.

"But that was over a year ago." he added, only just able to keep the bite from his tone.

Scarlet nodded, leaning back in her chair. The bunny had taken flight now. She was all lioness here, a queen in the heart of her territory, mistress of all she surveyed, and those hot, ice-blue eyes watched him keenly over her steepled fingers. "As you are aware, the role requires certain aptitudes. Qualities that are difficult to assess on a CV and in an interview. So, potential applicants are allocated a minor role in the company, then in due course, we allocate them a manufactured account to evaluate their performance."

"Hence Prometheus," Richard nodded, comprehension blooming. "Who seduced Zeus with plates of bones wrapped in fats to give offal covered beef to humanity."

"Then stole fire, and was punished by being chained to a rock for the great eagle to feast upon his liver each morning," Scarlet added.

"Very symbolic. So, if the candidate lacks the predisposition for the role, they're fed to the eagles?"

"More or less," she purred with a subtle tilt of her head that made Richard wonder if she wasn't entirely joking. "But, congratulations Dick, you've passed the test. Though I have to say, you were taking your sweet time about it. I was about ready to chuck your ass to the curb on general principle. Rather ironic, really. If you hadn't, you certainly would have been after I read what you sent me earlier. How long did all this take you?"

"About a day and a half," he shrugged, feeling very warm in his suit. It all made so much sense and was now so obvious. God, how could he have been so stupid? Russian organised crime. He must have lost his mind.

"Extraordinary. That's half as long as the last guy who passed the test." Shifting back in her chair and crossing her legs, revealing a lot of her soft, golden thigh, Scarlet brought a hand up to toy with a lock of her hair, studying him with renewed interest. "I must say, though, yours is certainly the most unique report yet. And all from the financial data you were provided and a bit of digging. Just extraordinary. You certainly have a vivid imagination for an accountant, Dick. You've been reading too much Andy McNab. Still, I might just have to commission you to write a novel." The corner of her mouth curled in the ghost of a smile and the tip of her pink tongue swept over her plump, juicy, pink lips. "A seedy little erotic thriller. Perhaps about a businessman caught cheating on his wife."

She let the suggestion hang there, but held his gaze just long enough for Richard's blood to turn to ice in his veins.

Shit.

Was it just a coincidence? Or did Scarlet know something? No, that was crazy. How could she? He was being silly. She couldn't know anything about him and Rebecca, unless- the sound he'd heard outside the office door. Someone moving around behind the door... Had it been Scarlet? Fuck.

"So... I'm getting promoted?"

Smooth, very smooth, asshole.

Whatever Scarlet had been expecting, that wasn't it. She laughed.

She actually laughed. A soft, kittenish, and unmistakably feminine sound, as fair to the ears as she was lovely to behold. It was the first time Richard had ever heard it and despite his rather precarious situation; it surprised him to find the sweet melody suited her and made her appear more delicate.

He almost forgot what a bitch she could be.

Almost.

"Not quite," she chuckled. "Consider it more of a lateral move. You'll remain in my department, but within a role more suited to your talents. Get a nice little pay raise, your own private office three doors down the hall. Just what you need, a little *privacy*..."

"Is that a prerequisite for the position?" Richard asked, his throat growing tighter.

She giggled softly. "In your case, Dick, I think it's indispensable."

She was baiting him, daring him to ask the question. Both manoeuvring and mocking him. Just another game. Fuck, fuck, fuck!

"If you say so," he said simply, sidestepping her trap by the skin of his teeth. *Great, now all I've got to do is get the hell out of Dodge.*

He just needed an excuse.

Just one polite reason to-

Scarlet's lips twisted wryly. "Very good Dick, but as much as I'd like to sit here engaging in a bit of witty repartee with you, I don't have the time and you don't have the wit, so why don't we just cut through the bullshit." She removed her glasses and placed them on the desk before turning her computer monitor around for him to see.

Oh shit…

A video file was open on the screen, paused for the moment, but Richard recognised it as the feed from a security camera, a camera from his office. The camera that just so happened to be looking down at his cubicle. Where he was sitting… with Rebecca in his lap.

How could he have forgotten about the damn cameras?

Scarlet clicked her tongue, the lioness's merciless blue eyes fixed on him. "Now Dick, I don't care what my staff get up to on their lunch. Frankly, if you're off the clock, I don't give a fuck… so long as it takes place off company property."

She clicked her mouse, and the feed started replaying the scene. There was no sound. The audio was redirected to a pair of buds in the jack, but then again, he didn't need it. Every moment was still seared in his memory. Him and Rebecca making out in his chair. The call from Alice. Rebecca hiding. His wife stripping on the screen while the girl sucked him off… Richard hated to admit it, but even under her scrutiny, the memory of it was making him hard.

"Off the record, I have to say, I'm impressed. I thought the pair of you were just a boring, straight-laced, middle-class couple. The sort that argues twice a week and fucks once every leap year. I certainly never would have guessed Alice had it in her. I mean, I always suspected she had a bit of a wild streak in her. All these stuck-up bitches do, but to actually Skype her man at work to have phone sex! Bravo. And as for you…" She shut down the media player and twisted the monitor back around to face her, her eyes bright and mocking. "Well, look at the cock on you. And while a hot bit of young ass blows you under the desk, as well. Never knew you had it in you, either. I thought that only happened in bad porn."

With a shudder of self-loathing at his treacherous loins, Richard met Scarlet's gaze. "And I never guessed you were such a voyeur. What do you do, sit around here watching us all day?"

"No, not unless I have due cause to check the feeds. And when I spotted your little friend going into one of my departments, then strutting by my office door with that 'cat that got the canary grin' on her face nearly half an hour later… Well, it wouldn't be very professional of me to just turn a blind eye. Who knew what she was getting up to, or rather, who was getting into her…" she chuckled mockingly. "You should thank me, Dick. If someone in security had seen this. Well, who knows how far it could have gone..." She let the point hang there to let his imagination do the rest.

"Is that what happened to you? Did one guard catch you having a bonk and run off to tell Daddy?" The words were out before he could stop himself.

"Excuse me?"

Shit, now he'd done it.

He gritted his teeth against another outburst and tried to look contrite. "Never mind, I-"

"No, go on, *Dick*," she said, raising a hand to stop him, her voice suddenly very still and deadly serious. "So just what are they all saying about me? I'm the office slut? A hot fuck in the closet, or a quick suck in the bog type of girl? Or is it the old chestnut, daddy issues? Sleeping with all of Daddy's little minions because old Walrus Face wouldn't buy her a pony for her tenth birthday?"

"No one said anything about a pony," he admitted, resisting the urge to look away as a chill crept up his spine and he had the unmistakable feeling of shrinking into his chair.

"Then you've missed some of the more lurid variations," she continued. "No Dick, I've never been caught on camera. I'm not a slut, *Dick*. I just like sex and I'm not afraid to show it. Or enjoy it."

Richard wondered for a moment if he should ask, but she spoke with such resolve, he couldn't help himself. "And the stories about you with Tommy Cox, and Mike from Legal."

She shrugged. "They're true. I found them attractive and thought they would be a decent lay. So, I offered, and they took me up on it. They were under no obligations."

Richard was aghast. "They lost their jobs and their wives divorced them because of your affairs. Doesn't that bother you?"

"No!" Scarlet held up a dismissive hand. "Their wives divorced them because they found out their husbands were getting some on the side and didn't like it. And I sacked them because they thought banging the boss's daughter whenever she needed to take the edge off gave them the right to talk shit about the company. Clearly, they were wrong. If their wives had sucked their dicks once in a while, maybe they would've gone home to them instead of meeting me in the Travel Lodge. So, what do I have to feel guilty about Dick? I'm not married and I'm not lying to my spouse to bang a hot bit of ass." Her smile dropped, and her expression was suddenly as cold and hard as a diamond. "It's rather hypocritical, don't you think, questioning my morals when you're the one getting a little lip service from your bit on the side?"

She had it right, of course. And whatever else his faults might have been, Richard wasn't so great a fool as to try lying to himself.

What right did he have to criticize her?

They may have both been indiscreet, but she was single and a free agent.

He, on the other hand, was a married man.

"Yes. You're right, I'm sorry, and it won't happen again," he capitulated and finally looked down at his feet, running a hand through his hair. Scarlet nodded, accepting his apologies, but it wasn't enough. He felt the need to say more, to explain himself, or perhaps just get it all out in the open. "This all started Friday night, after we got home from the party, and I let myself get carried away in the moment. I made a mistake and now- "

"Why?"

"What?" The question was so unexpected, he rounded on her without thinking.

Yet Scarlet merely looked back, nonplussed. Then, as if he hadn't spoken at all, she calmly pulled open one of her drawers and pulled out a Tupperware tub and a small packet of chocolate dip. "Do you mind? I had lunch but seem to have missed dessert, courtesy of your little show."

He nodded, but without waiting for his response, Scarlet had already stood up and was walking around the desk to sit on the edge directly in front of his chair. She crossed her legs. "So, why was it a mistake?"

"You have got to be joking," he stammered, all too aware of their closeness as the floral scent of her perfume fogged his senses.

"Am I laughing?" she asked, undoing the container's fastenings before carefully balancing the lid on her knee like a plate, then tipping a variable punnet of fat red strawberries out onto it. "If I were joking, Dick, you would be in stitches. Now, this girl-"

"Rebecca," he cut in, perhaps a little too forcefully, but he didn't care. He didn't want her referring to Rebecca in that way. Like she was insignificant.

Scarlet shot him a withering, almost pitying look as she ripped the lid off of her dip. "Okay, *Rebecca.* You've known her a while?"

Richard nodded. "Yeah, she lives in our building. She's our babysitter."

She exaggerated rolling her eyes, then plucked up one strawberry and plunged it in the dip. "I never would have guessed, still I suppose a cliché is a cliché for a reason. Okay, so you've known her a while. And she comes from a troubled home?"

"Y-you could say that," he trailed off for a second as he watched her bring the fruit up to her lips, her tongue sliding out to taste the chocolate. He forced himself to look away, his eyes quickly fixing on a point out the window. There wasn't anywhere else he could look. Her perch on the desk caused the already tiny skirt to rise higher while placing the swells of her breasts just at his eye level…

"Abuse?"

"Something like that. Her old man isn't much cop with men, but he can be a hard one with women."

"You sound like you don't like him." She bit down on the berry and moaned a low sound of pleasure that seemed to thrum down his spine, all the way to the base of his cock.

"We've had words." Actually, Richard had caught the little bastard threatening to beat his daughter black and blue after he'd had a few too many, and she'd come home late. So he had explained, from one father to another, that that wasn't any way to treat his daughter.

The guy had gotten the message, at least for a while. However, the sounds from their flat had been growing more and more volatile recently. No doubt he would have to reiterate that little lesson before long.

She popped the rest of the strawberry into her mouth, her tongue skimming out to lick up the single roll of sweetness that was creeping down her chin. "And I suppose her mum just sits there and lets him bully her around?"

"No, her mother buggered off and left her alone with the short-arse, went to live with a boyfriend in Leeds or Bradford or somewhere up North. Rebecca hasn't seen or spoken to her in years."

She pondered that for a moment, before picking up another strawberry and nibbling it thoughtfully. "No other family?"

"None," he swallowed, his mouth and throat growing dry as the office seemed to grow hotter by the second.

"Then I don't see the problem," she declared, then slowly took the whole berry into her mouth. "She seems smart enough, enough not to think you'll leave your wife for her. She's just confused, as most girls her age are. I dare say you're the strongest male role model she's ever had and can't quite work out how she feels about you. Give her a few weeks to work it out, and she'll meet some boy her own age. But if you tell her it was all a mistake, you'll probably just do more harm than good for the poor girl."

"And what about Alice?"

"Do you love her?" She forewent the fruit entirely this time and dipped her finger into the dip.

"Of course I do, but-"

"Would you leave her for this girl or try to lead either of them on?" Scarlet put her chocolate-covered finger into her mouth and sucked it clean with a long slow draw that had Richard's fists clenching in his lap.

"Never," he rasped, his gaze focusing on those pouting pink lips, and for the briefest moment, he wondered what that lush mouth would look like wrapped around his dick.

She shrugged. "Then? What about her? Sex isn't a luxury, Dick. It's a necessity. The body needs it like it needs food and water. If you're not getting any at home, then you need to look for it elsewhere. If having a little on the side gets the urge out of your system, just enjoy the adventure while it lasts."

"Spoken like a woman who's never been married."

Scarlet smirked triumphantly and gestured at him with another plump strawberry. "And who never wants to. Humans aren't monogamous by nature, so why should I be? Just because society demands it? I'm a girl with needs who doesn't like to be tied down, and matrimony is one big leash, Dick, especially when there are so many men out there I haven't tried yet."

She dunked half the berry into the dip. "Besides, what good would telling her do? Cheaters say being honest is the right thing to do, but all they really want is to make themselves feel better about fucking up. She'll be happier not knowing."

"It's still wrong."

"How so? Is it wrong to grab a bite on the way home even though your wife is cooking dinner? No. You're hungry, so you eat. Why should sex be any different?" Her eyes then sparkled with mischief as she nibbled along the chocolate. "If it bothers you so much, just grow a pair and tell her. Or try for a three-way?"

"Now I know you're joking."

"Why not? It would certainly solve all your problems," she teased, stretching out one long graceful leg, the toe of her high-heel shoe, white to match her dress, brushing along his thigh and down his leg. "And it's certainly not adultery if your wife's banging her, too."

"Except Alice would cut my balls off and wear them as earrings," he breathed, forcing himself to look into her eyes, refusing to look down, all too aware of the unobstructed view she was offering him. Sharon Stone couldn't have done it better herself.

Holding his gaze, she leant forward until they were almost nose to nose. "I don't know. From what I saw, she's definitely full of surprises. It's always the up-tight ones that you've got to watch."

"Drop it Scarlet," he warned, gritting his teeth, his dick hard and tight and impossible to ignore.

"Am I right, Dick? I am, aren't I? Yeah, I bet she turns into a little nympho the moment her hair comes down." She dropped the plate of strawberries on the desk and reached out to finger his tie.

"Scarlet… I'm warning you." His throat was tight around the words as his heart pounded in his ears. Shit, he needed to get out of here. She was too close, he couldn't think, couldn't breathe, her damn perfume was fogging his head.

Damnit, why did she have to smell so good…

"Mmm… you know you're cute when you're flustered." She closed the gap, sliding off the desk and onto his lap so the crotch of her dress pressed against his cock through his trousers. "Come on, Dick, don't be greedy. She'll love going down on your little babysitter while you fuck her like a bitch in hea-"

Her taunt died in a surprised gasp as he seized a fistful of her blonde hair.

Chapter Six

"Shut up."

"Dick!" Scarlet hissed. "W-what're you doing?"

"I said, shut your fucking mouth." His voice was low and deathly calm, a cocktail of anger and lust pulsing through him like nitro-glycerine. Richard lurched to his feet, towering over her…

Except Scarlet wasn't a woman to be dominated.

She was a fighter.

She'd fought every day of her life. Against her brothers, against peers who thought her beneath them, against subordinates and superiors alike who thought of her as an entitled and a spoiled brat. It was why she had fought so hard to graduate top of her class at Cambridge. Why she had taken this entry-level role in her father's company and would work her way to the very top, rather than just let him marry her off.

She wouldn't be cowed or humbled or let any man take advantage of her.

The moment her feet touched the ground, she pivoted, twisting free of his grip, her arm sweeping out, nails hooked to claw his face. She attacked with all the swiftness and ferocity of a cornered cat.

However, Richard was faster, twisting out of her reach, grabbing her wrist and dragging it around behind her back, forcing her down across the desk. Before she could fully comprehend what just happened, he was leaning over her, caging her there, pinned against the desk, his body deliciously hard beneath his suit.

"Scream, and I'll gag you," he warned, fettering both her wrists in one hand while the other tugged at his tie, loosening the noose.

"You wouldn't dare." Scarlett shot him an angry look over her shoulder, even as the raw emotion in his voice made her knees weak. No man, or woman for that matter, had ever been this way with her. She'd never known getting dominated could be such a turn on.

Who'd of ever guessed he had it in him?

Richard stared her down, his gaze fixed on that pretty little mouth of hers, her luscious lips just the right size and shape for sucking cock. He was sorely tempted to gag her anyway on principle alone, but he had a better idea.

He was sick of all her bullshit, her teasing, her constant shots at Alice. He might have fucked up, possibly ruined his marriage, his life, and be about to fuck up his career a whole lot more, but that didn't give her the right to belittle his wife. This time, she'd gone too far.

It was time to teach the *Tight Ass Bitch* a lesson.

"Wouldn't I?" A dark grin pulled at the corner of his mouth as he pulled the tie over his head and looped it round Scarlet's wrists in a simple slip knot. "You've been a very bad girl, Scarlet. Do you know what I do with bad girls?" He drew back to stand over her, one hand braced against the small of her back, holding her and her wrists down, the other pushing up her skirt, bearing the lush curves of her naked derriere.

"What?" she gasped, shaking, heat and embarrassment crackling through her, making it impossible for her to stay still.

"This." His hand swept down, slapping her right cheek with a loud crack. "I give them a spanking."

Scarlet couldn't help giving a little gasp. It didn't hurt, not really, but the hot sting made her clit pulse within its hood and she twisted against her bonds, trying to give the little bud some much-needed attention. "*Dick...* I'm your boss-ah!"

He smacked her ass again, the left cheek this time, and *harder*.

"No, Scarlet," he growled, trying to ignore the way her lovely derriere, now marred by a pair of red handprints, was wriggling against the bulge of his cock. Damnit, had she noticed? This would all be for nought if she knew she was affecting him too. He reinforced the assertion with another slap that actually made her jump. "You're a bad girl. Say it."

"No." Scarlet shook her head, but when the blow came, the delicious slap of skin meeting skin and the explosion of heat was too much. She bit her lip to hold the moan at bay, but there was no stopping the slickness between her thighs.

"Say it."

Slap!

"I-I…"

Slap!

"Say it!"

Slap!

"I'm a bad girl!" she moaned, the words flowing from her as thick and sweet as honeyed cream. God, why did it have to feel so good?

Richard raised his hand, then held it there. "Again."

"Mmm… I'm a bad, bad girl!" Biting her lower lip, Scarlet chanced a glance back, her eyes pleading, but for what? Mercy, or perhaps another smack.

His hand dropped to brush over her buttocks. She instinctively flinched away from his touch but relaxed when his fingers began kneading her backside, massaging away the heat. "You admit you've been bad?"

"Yes… very… mmm… bad…" Scarlet purred, pushing back against his hand as he made larger and larger circles. She was so turned on, so wet. What was he doing to her? Why was he making her so horny?

"Teasing me. Trying to seduce me. Belittling my wife." His hand slid down between her legs, fingers reaching, feeling, sliding along her wetness, pushing through her grasping heat.

"Yes!" Scarlet gasped, her whole world shrinking down to the feeling of his finger filling her, stroking her delicate inner tissues, swirling and stirring her into wild delirium. Greedy for more, she wriggled and circled against his swirling digit, spreading her legs wider, opening for him.

"That's it, you bad girl, and who's the boss now?"

She swallowed, her body clenching around the digit, the tension building inside her. "You are."

"Again," he growled, curling his finger to brush over that patch of rough tissue under her clit while thrumming the bundle of nerves with the pad of his thumb.

Scarlet gasped, her eyes widening as a fog settled over her thoughts. Sensation rippled outward from wherever he touched, only threatening to crash over her, driving her to the brink. Just not over it. It was the sweetest torture, the cruellest ecstasy.

No one had ever done this to her before, made her feel so vulnerable. It was delicious. "You... You're the boss... *Richard!*"

He couldn't remember the last time she'd used his Christian name. And the way she said it, so pleading and desperate, had his lips twisting in a dark grin before he leant down over her to lick the shell of her ear. "Good girl." He withdrew his finger.

Panic flaring inside her, she twisted right and left, trying to grab his hand, but the tie held strong. "No! Don't stop...!" She yelped as he swatted her arse again, the sting dissolving into delicious throbbing pleasure.

"Are you talking back to me? Bad girl," He growled, his tone low and primal, all but tearing at his belted trousers to liberate his cock. Taking himself in hand, he rubbed the crown along her slick, greedy cleft, the tip sliding through her swollen folds to graze her little bundle of nerves, making her shudder and gasp.

"No… please… Sir… mmm… don't stop… feels so good… I…" Panting, her pussy hot and throbbing, begging, no *demanding* more, Scarlet pressed back, circling her hips, desperate to feel him slid inside her, filling her, pounding her.

It did no good. He had her pinned to her desk, caged by his body, hands bound, completely at his mercy, and it only made her burn hotter.

"What? What do you want, Scarlet?"

"*Please…*" she heard herself beg. Her throat tightened around the word as she turned to look back over her shoulder at *him*.

This couldn't be the man she knew.

Her subordinate, dependable Richard Martin. The quiet, mild-mannered guy who never gave her a second look. That guy was fun to tease and torment, but did nothing for her, despite his thick dark hair, chiselled bone structure and broad build.

This man, who was now almost nose to nose with her, was different. Everything about him excited her. The way he looked at her, handled her, and just completely dominated her.

God, this couldn't be happening. Who was this man? What was he doing to her? She didn't do things like this, never at work, and she was never submissive in sex.

She needed control. Her lovers were quiet and submissive, little more than tools for her pleasure, dildos with a pulse. They couldn't make her beg.

Yet this man had. And fuck, why did it feel so good?

"Louder," Richard pressed, enjoying the moment, relishing the turnaround, the power. He loved hearing her like this. So desperate and needy. All her poise and professionalism stripped away to leave just the raging wanton.

She licked her lips, her eyes smouldering, dark with desire. Needing to move, to take some control, she curled her hips, desperate to stroke her clit against his crest and ease the throbbing ache pulsing there. "Please!"

"Please what?" he asked, the deep growl of his tone sending hot shivers through her core as, bending his knees, he lined himself up, the broad tapered head of his cock nestling between her folds. Just one push and he would be buried inside her.

Scarlet couldn't bear it.

"Fuck me… please, fuck me-oh!" Scarlet gasped, her eyes widening and mouth falling open in a long moan as his hips snapped forward, driving in deep. The delicious shock of his cock sliding home rushed over her, making her head spin.

Too deep. Oh God, he's huge. How the hell does Alice ever ride this beast?

"Yeah, is this what you want, Scarlet?" he rasped in a low and sultry voice that just screamed sex. His hands dropped to her hips, fingers squeezing hard enough for her to feel the bite, both dragging her back and tilting her at just the right angle to take him. Not so much holding her as using her body to fuck her back onto his cock.

"Oh yes… oh yes… yes Sir!" she panted, her insides clenching, squeezing all around him, pleasure rippling out to her fingers and toes as she felt herself open to him, inch by sinfully thick, hard inch of him. Fuck, she'd never dreamed someone could fill her so completely. "Oh fuck… oh my God… yes… make me take it. I've been such a horrible boss, I need to be punished… mmm… punish that pussy with your big fucking dick!"

Richard was more than happy to oblige. "Don't worry, you're going to get everything you deserve."

Fuck, what the hell was wrong with him? He didn't dominate his lovers, didn't degrade or overpower them. This wasn't him. He'd never been like this with Alice, hadn't been like it with Rebecca… but he liked it.

"Just look at you, you bad girl. Getting fucked across your desk with your hands tied behind your back. Your snug little cunt milking my cock. You're just bloody loving this, aren't you?"

It was time to teach his boss's daughter a lesson.

She had been asking for this, well now it was time she learned to be careful what she wished for.

"Yes! Yes, I love it!" Scarlet moaned, writhing in his arms as his hips curled against her derriere. There was a momentary feeling of emptiness as he pulled back before his hands snapped her back to meet his hard thrust, making her feel every hard inch of his godly cock driving her up onto her tiptoes.

The feeling was so intense. She felt so stretched. So full.

It made her whole core pulse and tingle, and clench around him, but it was too late. He was already sliding out, almost all the way, then driving into her again, and again, until he was pounding into her greedy sex. "I'm a bad little whore… bad fucking whore… pound that pussy… it's yours- oh- oh God, yes, yes!

The orgasm came out of nowhere, rushing over her, leaving her a limp, shaking mess. He fucked her through it, drawing out her pleasure and driving her down into the desk so that her heavy breasts and stiff aching peaks dragged across the wood through her silky blouse. His body bore down on her, pinning her there so all she could do was struggle against the silk binding her wrists in a desperate need to grab something. the desk, him, anything that might give her a little leverage.

She shouldn't have liked it, but she did.

She never would have thought she could enjoy sex restrained, but this feeling of being under his control, powerless, at his mercy.

It was dark, primitive and so wild.

He knew just how to treat her.

He was splitting her open. Using her like a bitch in heat, and it was such a turn on.

She couldn't bear it. She needed to grab something, anything…

"Yeah, that's it, cum for me, you bad girl, cum all over my cock… mmm… spread that ass for me, show me your pretty little hole," Richard growled, drinking in the sight of Scarlet's bound hands grabbing her smooth alabaster cheeks, those perfectly manicured nails biting into the soft skin, spreading them wide to show him the tight rosebud nestled within.

The vision sent a hot shiver of lust down his spine, and he couldn't resist brushing it with his thumb, circling the sphincter, pushing in ever so slightly.

Scarlet could only gasp at the feeling against her pucker, the sensation causing her sex to clench around him. "Yes Sir… please, punish me, I need it… I… I…"

"As you wish."

He growled and Scarlet could have screamed as he pulled out.

Then his arms were around her and she came up and away from the desk. Then, as if she were as light as a feather, he hoisted her to her feet and walked her around the desk to the window.

"Put your hands on the glass," Richard instructed, the tie coming undone with a quick tug.

"What?" she asked, looking out the window, down across the canal, and the bustling hive of activity that was Gloucester Docks, where the whole of the city seemed to be wandering amongst bright colourful stalls.

He couldn't be serious. All it would take was just one person looking up and-

"Do it," he urged, slapping her ass again, the crack as sharp as a bullwhip and the sting enough to overwhelm caution.

She did as he commanded, bending forward slightly and pressing both hands against the window, the glass misting with her breath. "Good, now stay right where you are."

"What!" she snapped, her heart pounding in her breast. "Are you mad? The market's down there... someone might see, *Sir*."

"And I bet that gets you wet," he retorted, crouching down and nudging her thighs further apart so the musky scent of her sex fogged his thoughts. "Mmm... your cunt's all pink and slick and begging me to keep fucking her."

"No, Dick, please, that's... not fair. I don't- oh!"

He pushed a finger along her swollen folds, through her slick cream and into her lush depths, all the way to the knuckle. "Your dripping, you bad girl. Say it."

"No, please..." she panted, biting her lip to keep from moaning at the tingling shooting through her core. However, there was no resisting the choked sob as the digit twisted and curled, feeling and rubbing all of her most sensitive places at once. Nor could Scarlet stop herself from pushing back against him, her sex clenching. "Mmm... No! Wait, not here, there are so many people down there, what if someone looks up, they could see- "

"So what?" Removing his finger, he reached out and took her last few strawberries from the desk, crushing them to a juicy pulp in his hand. "Let them look, go on, let them see you for the little slut you are. Let the *whole damn city* see you for who you really are," he said, before putting his hand on her inner thigh.

"Stop... You can't... I'll scream..." Scarlet gasped, shaking as her clit pulsed at the feeling of his hand and the illicitness of the strawberry juice sliding over her skin, spreading it up her leg and over her butt. Then, it wasn't just his hands.

"Go ahead, scream all you want, that'll just make everyone look, won't it?" Richard said, following the sticky trail with his tongue, greedily licking up both the sweetness of the fruit and the salty flavour of her desire. "Maybe even someone in the office will hear and come running. Wouldn't that be something? Is that what you want, Scarlet? To prove all those dirty gossips, right?"

"No," Scarlet choked out, shaking, the throbbing of her core growing ever stronger as the slick glide of his tongue swept up her inner thigh.

"Then shut the fuck up before I gag that pretty mouth of yours," Richard barked, before pivoting and covering her swollen clit with the lush heat of his mouth.

Scarlet couldn't stand it.

His words were so dirty and crude, raw with lust. No one had ever spoken to like that.

It was such a fucking turn on.

She couldn't bear it. Just keeping her hands on the glass was torture in itself. She wanted to grab him, fist his hair, sit on his face, squeeze her tits, rub her clit, something, anything to-

"Oh… Oh my God… oh fuck-yes!" She gasped and moaned, squeezing her eyes shut against the feeling of sensory overload as he sucked hard and greedily on her little bud before lashing it with his tongue.

"You want to get caught, don't you? Yeah, I know you do. Your pussy's so juicy. Just the thought of it has your greedy little cunt all soaked. Don't pretend you don't like it. You're dripping for it…"

"No… *Dick*!… that's not- don't say things like that! Mmm… I can't help it… you're making me… oh no, no, please, if you do that… I'll…"

She was shaking, the waves of sensation crashing over her so violently her legs were in danger of giving way from under her as her fingers clawed the window for something, anything, to hold on to.

However, Richard showed no mercy.

"You'll what? Go on Scarlet, tell me," he pressed, swirling his tongue around the bundle of nerves, his hands fastening to her quivering hips, dragging them closer…

"I'll- oh fuck… oh my God… I'll… I'll…" She was mindless with the raw need to cum. And so close, when his tongue suddenly abandoned her clit to drag along her folds, the world shattered around her. "Oh God, yes, yes, fuck yes, I'm cumming, I'm cumming, I'm cumming, fuck, fuck…"

Richard tongued her through the climax, not stopping even as her hips trembled in his arms. For what he had in mind, he wanted her good and relaxed. "Yeah, that's it, go on Scarlet, cum for me, let the whole damn city see you cum!"

She bowed her head to press her forehead against the window as the waves crashed over her, the glass deliciously cold against her flushed skin. "No… please… why are you doing this to me, please, I can't take it- oh fuck, yes, yes!"

"Mmm… beg all you want, Scarlet, this is the mouth that doesn't lie." Deaf to her pleas, he buried his face in her cleft, devouring her with long deep licks, his tongue swirling while the rough of his jaw scrapped oh so deliciously along her inner thighs. "You love it. Say it."

Scarlet shook her head, but the words stuck in her throat. She was shaking, powerless against the urge to grind back onto his tongue as her clit pulsed and throbbed, pleading for just that little bit of attention to send her soaring to the starry heavens. "No! Please don't make me- oh fuck, oh fuck, okay, okay, yes, I love it, I love it! Use me, abuse me… please, please, please, I'm your naughty little fuck toy… oh God… that's your pussy, that's your pussy…"

His cock jumped at her wanton tone, but Richard pushed on regardless.

Not yet. She wasn't ready yet. Just a little more…

"So now you don't want me to stop?" he asked with a mock teasing tone, pulling back just enough to drag the flat of his tongue along her folds, from clit to base, then back again in longer and longer glides.

A shudder wracked Scarlet at the suggestion. Or perhaps it was another orgasm. "No, no, don't stop, don't stop, please, put your dick back in me, fuck me against the glass for the whole world to see, make me cum all over your big hard cock."

"No," he rasped, his tone low and primal as he worked his tongue higher, hands spreading her cheeks. "I'm not done with you yet."

"What-oh!" Scarlet gasped as warmth washed over her pucker, sending shivers racing up her spine and throwing fresh fuel on the already raging lusts. Then his tongue slid up to circle her virgin hole, teasing it with gently prods and flicks.

No one had ever done anything like this to her before. It felt strange, dirty and wrong, but so exciting. "Wait! No… no, not there, please- oh fuck!"

She panted, her back curling at the feeling of his tongue pushing through her tight ring of muscle. Then her mind went blank, consumed by the sensation of wet heat sliding in and out.

"Wow Scarlet, I've barely started rimming you and you're already drenching the floor. Who would have ever guessed you were such an anal whore, and in front of the whole city, you bad girl." He swatted her arse just hard enough for the pain to heighten the pleasure. "Just look at you, you're loving this, aren't you?"

"Yes! Yes, I'm a bad girl, your bad little slut, punish my little hole, I deserve to be punished… I deserve it… I… I-"

"Have the tastiest ass," Richard growled, leaning over her, his body caging her against the glass as powerful fingers fisted in her hair and dragged her head round. Then he took her mouth in a bruising kiss, his sinful tongue encircling hers, brushing and stroking and fogging her thoughts with his strong, heady flavour.

No, not his flavour, hers. He was forcing her to taste herself.

The revelation made her core clench at the very moment he slid inside her.

"Mmm… I could fuck your cunt all day, you bad girl," Richard groaned, his dick painfully hard and the temptation to give himself over to the feeling of his lush walls milking him was almost irresistible. Almost. Instead, he rolled his hips, stirring her grasping sheath before pulling out, his shaft slick and glistening with her cream.

Scarlet shuddered at the loss and made a pouting sound that dissolved into a low moan as he leant down to nibble the shell of her ear, hands dropping to her naked ass, spreading her cheeks for his cock to glide up, the broad crest parting her folds.

She was shaking, so on edge, her whole body was almost humming with carnal need. One little push would be all it took to push her over the edge-

"But now…" he whispered in her ear, pausing only to bite down and tug on her lobe. "I want to find out how tight your ass really is."

She stilled at the dark promise in his voice, eyes widening as the crown touched her pucker.

"Wait, you don't mean? Oh no…" she gasped, shaking her head.

"Oh yes, your ass is mine," he growled, rearing back to drink in the vision of her stretched out before him. Flushed and panting, her blonde hair had become a passionate mess and that once immaculate white business dress was rumpled the way that only a good, hard fucking could do, its skirt scrunched up around her hips to show off the full curves of her luscious, strawberry smeared butt.

It was a complete contrast from the woman he knew and filled him with a savage, primitive pride. He slid forward, pressing his slick tip against the ring of muscle. Soft and pliant from the multiple orgasms, her body opened before him.

"Oh fuck! Oh, fuck!" Scarlet gasped, her eyes going wide at the sudden burning sensation, the feeling of something hard, thick, and slick splitting her open. Instinctively, she tried to clench down, to force him back, but that only seemed to speed his invasion on, so the broad crest slid through.

"That's it Scarlet, let me in… mmm you really are a tight arsed bitch all right, but don't worry, not for much longer," Richard promised, curling his hips in small circles, trying to resist the feeling of her body wrapping around his crown, sucking him in. He needed to loosen her up first, or else this would hurt.

Scarlet could only groan. Somewhere, deep down and far away, a little voice was screaming for her to give herself over to him, to let it come, but she couldn't. She just… couldn't. He was too big. Too thick.

She'd never felt this full, so stretched. So…

She threw a look back over her shoulder at him, her blue eyes large and pleading. "S-sir, I…"

Their eyes met and she couldn't keep her gasp at bay at the wild look burning in his eyes, the warring emotions battling just beneath the surface. It was the most savage look she'd ever seen, the reflection of the beast that lurked in the heart of every man as he was visibly torn between restraint, and the instinctive desire to fuck, to rut and claim her as his bitch.

His grip on her tightened, the fingers biting into her hips, holding her still as he took a step forward, pressing her to the glass while his dick kept working back and forth, slick with their mixed juices, sending heat rushing through her.

"No, Scarlet, look straight ahead."

She obeyed, too far gone now to turn back.

Overhead, the sky had turned a deep lilac, slashed with shades of pink and orange that danced across the waters of the canal as the sun slipped away behind the horizon. Below, the fair was still in full swing and growing busier as people finished their work and came to browse amongst the stalls. Anyone could look up and see them.

Someone already was.

Her reflection stared back at her from the window, but with the face of a stranger, with flushed skin and a hooded gaze, framed by a dishevelled mess of spun gold.

Bent at the waist, she looked shameless, like a whore just begging to be fucked.

The sight was so erotic, she couldn't bear it and tried squeezing her eyes shut against the image, but it lingered, burned into her mind.

"No, watch Scarlet, I want you to see," Richard bit out, his voice low and so dark with lust that she couldn't resist. Her eyes locked to his in the glass, and his hips snapped forward, driving his cock into her heat.

"Oh!" she gasped, fighting the urge to close her eyes against the sudden rush of hot sensations. "Oh fuck… oh fuck… You're… you're in my ass… there's a dick in my… oh God, this feels so…." She could feel herself opening to take him all the way, her forbidden little hole stretching to fit him, and only him.

Richard pulled back slowly, letting half of his length slide out, then drove back in, drawing another ragged sound from Scarlet. It was a deliciously snug fit, with her inner walls wrapping around him like a fist in a warm velvet glove, squeezing him tight, trying to milk the cum right out of him with every stroke.

"Yeah… you like it, don't you?" His voice was thick and gruff, more beast than man. With each push and slide, his hands dragged her into the saddle of his hips, inch by hard throbbing inch until he was balls deep.

"Yes!" she gasped, surrendering to the sinfully wicked sensations rippling out from her ass, making her clit throb and nipples ache. "Oh my fucking God… this feeling, it's so… so intense, I- I love it…. don't stop, don't stop…"

"Don't worry, you bad girl, I won't stop…" he promised, his eyes drifting down to watch his dick sliding in and out of her forbidden little hole. "Yeah, that's it, mmm… goddamn, you're taking it up the ass like a proper little whore now."

"Oh God, yes… yes Sir, I'm your whore, please, fuck me, harder, make me feel every inch of that big cock pounding my tight little virgin ass." Not caring if they were discovered, she pushed against the window to meet each thrust, grinding herself back onto his cock.

"And whose ass is this, my little whore?"

The words came unbidden.

"It's yours, all yours. I'm your good little anal whore. Split me open on your dick, make me take it. I love your cock in all my holes!"

"All of them? Even this tight little virgin ass?" he grunted, the slap of flesh meeting flesh rising around them, his movements growing more urgent with the feeling of his release building.

She bowed her head, pressing her brow to the window, the glass deliciously cool against her flushed skin. "Yes! All of them! I love taking it up the ass for you.

I'm your naughty little office whore, that just another whole for you, only you- oh fuck, oh fuck, Sir, please!"

"Please what?"

He was close, so fucking close. Not sure how much longer he could last, he pushed one hand down beneath the folds of her skirt, into the bounty of lush, wet heat. He was close, but so was she. He could feel it and rubbed her clit while fucking her with a single-minded need to make her cum just once more.

"Punish me. Sir, please punish me, I deserve it! Punish me, punish all of my holes every day." Scarlet couldn't breathe, couldn't think, she could only feel. Feel the heat and fullness moving through her ass, the waves crashing over her as rough fingers strummed her throbbing clit and turned her legs to jelly. "My ass is yours, all yours whenever you want… fuck, I'm gonna cum, oh fuck, oh fuck, I'm gonna cum on your cock, oh my fuckin… yes, yes, make me cum on your fucking cock! Fuck that ass, it's yours, all fucking yours, oh fuck, oh fuck, I'm cumming, I'm fucking cumming! I'm-oh!"

Her orgasm exploded through her, unlike any release that had come before, sending her soaring. Then she started to shake as the aftershocks claimed her, and Richard couldn't resist the feeling of her ripple around his thick, swollen cock.

"Yeah, that's it you naughty whore, cum for me, cum for me in front of the whole goddamn city- ah shit, I'm cumming too!"

He moaned, burying his cock in her one last time as he came, hard. Hard enough for small black spots to dance before his eyes.

Amidst the fog of her climax, Scarlet felt his release like a flood of heat deep inside her. It was the first time a man had ever come inside her, and she liked it.

He'd stained her, branded her with a mark that could never be erased.

It made her feel dirty, deliciously dirty.

She wanted more.

Chapter Seven

For the longest moment, Richard just watched Scarlet, the beast in him wanting to savour its victory, burning the sight of her stretched out beneath him into his memory.

Then the moment passed, and it plunged him face first into cold reality.

Oh fuck…

Scarlet looked back at him over her shoulder, her full lips half curling with that damn mocking smirk. "Mmm… was I a good little whore for you, Dick?"

"Knock it off, this… this was a mistake." He stepped back and quickly shoved himself into his trousers.

She cooed and wiggled her ass, her rosebud agape and weeping pearl tears. "*Aww…* what's the matter *Dick,* the bitch going to throw a fit if you're late?" Her eyes flashed, daring him to bite.

"Fuck you," he snapped, resisting the sudden urge to put her over his knee, his nose wrinkling as his fingers fumbled with his belt buckle.

She straightened up and turned to face him, but made no effort to straighten the skirt still hitched about her hips. "We already played that game, remember?"

She lightly teased the petals of her sex with a finger before bringing the shiny digit to her lips.

"Yeah, well, maybe I'd rather forget." He wheeled around and walked around the desk, refusing to watch, and doing his best to ignore the still obvious stiffness straining against his trouser leg.

No, he wouldn't be tempted again.

However, Scarlet would not be dismissed so easily. Coming up behind him from the desk's other side, she slid her hands around his waist to finger his shirt buttons while rising up on her tiptoes to nip his ear. "Aww… don't be like that, lover. Come on, why don't you let me take care of that for you? You don't really want to go back to Alice smelling like sex, do you? There's a private washroom and shower in Daddy's office. I could wash your back for you and-"

"Forget it Scarlet!" Richard snapped. Angry and tired of her games, he brushed her hands away and rounded on her, so they were almost nose to nose. "This never happened, got it."

Scarlet held her ground, however, her playfulness gone, melted away to reveal an expression as cool and hard as ice. All except her eyes. They burned hot and fierce. "Don't kid yourself, Dick, that was the fuck of the century, and you know it. How long has it been since Alice fucked you like that? You think your little shop girl can?" Her smile spread wide, as cruel and sharp as a knife. "You're going to want it again."

She was right. About everything.

He wanted her. How could he not? He was only a man of flesh and blood, while she was the boss's daughter.

A young woman with a future as bright as her past was murky, a beautiful girl who played men the way a croupier dealt cards.

She was intelligent, sexy, and a damn great fuck.

She was Scarlet Holmes, his rock bottom, and he'd hit it hard, in more ways than one.

Now it was time to pick himself back up again.

So he turned his back on her and walked to the office door. Pulling it open, he didn't bother to look back. "Goodnight Scarlet."

At his back, still where she had stood, he could practically hear Scarlet seething when she hissed at his back. "I always get what I want, *Dick*."

It was the first time he had ever heard her composure crack.

He knew he should keep walking, to just let it slide, but sometimes he just couldn't help himself. "Then why don't you go up to your dad's office and fuck him instead?"

"Suck my clit you son of a- "

He pulled the door shut on her rebuff, and something smacked against the door. Something heavy.

Well, there goes my lateral move…

When he arrived home, the flat was dark and quiet.

It was only a short walk from the Docks, but he'd taken a detour to the 24-hour gym in the Gloucester Quay's, for a quick shower. Free membership was one perk of working for Holmes & Raine, and Scarlet had been right. He certainly didn't want to go home reeking of sex.

Freshly washed but still none the wiser as to what he was about to say or do, he'd practically dragged his feet all the way home. By the time he arrived at the tower block, the sun had long since gone down. Alice's car was in its usual parking spot, but a quick glance at the dark living room confirmed there was no sign of her inside. Nor Alexander.

He checked his phone to see if she'd tried to message him, but the screen stayed blank. The battery had died.

"Shit," he cursed quietly, the discovery winding his guts into a tighter string of knots. He'd been so out of it recently; he couldn't even remember when he'd last charged the phone. God only knew when the thing had died on him.

Had something happened to her? What if she or little Alex had had to be rushed to hospital? What if...

What if something hadn't happened...

What if she'd got worried because he was so late and tried to call him? What if, when he hadn't answered, she'd decided to check on him?

Just the prospect sent a cold shiver down his spine.

Had she seen them in the window? He'd been half expecting to get his collar felt the moment he'd left the building. Anyone could have seen and reported them to the police. Or perhaps he just missed her when he left the building and she'd run into Scarlet.

He had to know. He needed to speak to her. Maybe there was still time to – *what the fuck!*

He flipped on the living room light, about to plug the phone into the charging outlet there, when he heard it. A moan. Low and husky and *very* familiar.

Then the sound of wood creaking.

Bed springs squeaking

Someone calling.

Calling her name.

Then he was running through the room and down the hall to *their* bedroom door. A hard kick sent it swinging inward, and he stopped dead, his eyes widening at the sight of the bodies tangled together on the bed.

Alice... and Rebecca!

Coming soon… The Final

Temptation

L.M. MOUNTFORD

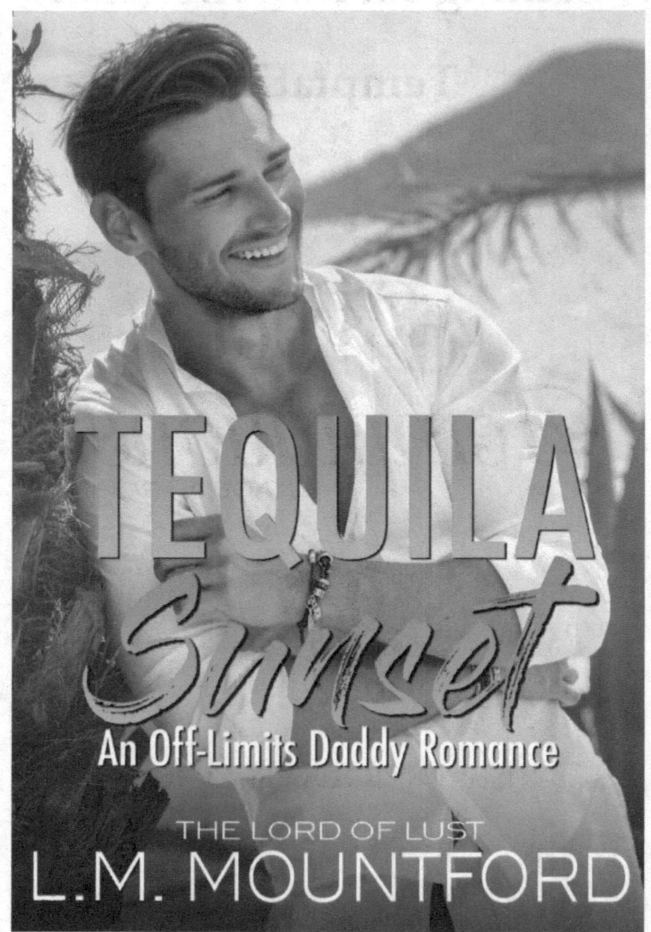

TEQUILA
Sunset
An Off-Limits Daddy Romance
THE LORD OF LUST
L.M. MOUNTFORD

TEQUILA Sunset

An Off-Limits Daddy Romance

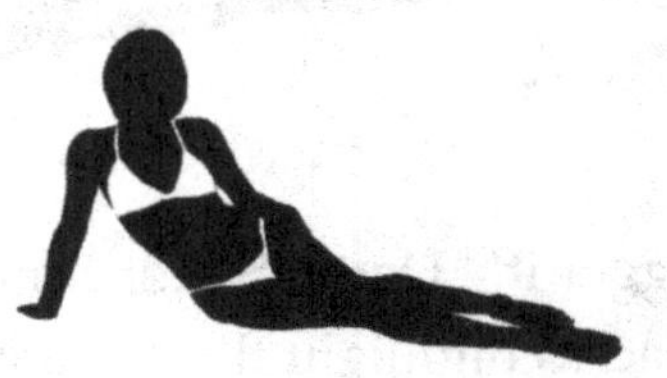

THE LORD OF LUST
L.M. MOUNTFORD

Chapter One

"Oh, bugger it!" David Street cursed, using his laptop's touchpad to highlight the paragraph he'd just written, and then deleting it with a tap of the key, collapsing back into his desk chair. He couldn't believe it. After working on it all morning, he was actually two paragraphs *behind* where he'd started.

He glowered at the screen, the cursor mocking his ineptitude with its constant blinking on the blank Word document.

A lot was made of the blank page. It was often said to taunt writers, to intimidate them with the immense space to fill. He never saw it that way, however. To him, the page wasn't a weight tugging him down. It was a challenge to overcome, fresh clay to be moulded however he saw fit.

No, the page wasn't the problem.

It was the pressure. The drive to outdo himself. To make this chapter better than the last. For the book to be new and exciting in a world where the well of creativity had run dry.

And time was running out.

His agent had been on the phone only that morning to tell him the publishers were getting impatient. That he had missed his deadline, and they wanted to see something by the end of the week or they would insist on the return of his advance.

"Bloody ingrates," he scoffed, leaning so far back in his chair until he was in real danger of falling on his arse. "You make them millions one day and they're kissing your ass. But one little bit of block the next, and it's *'hasta la vista, baby'*." He emphasised the Schwarzenegger impression by shooting a finger pistol at the ceiling before a scream, then a splash, had him on his feet and looking out the office's window.

Below, his daughter, Stacey, lay out on one of two inflatable beds drifting along the surface of the villa's large pool, sunning herself while her friend Cassandra swam lengths.

The girls spent most of the week like that. Enjoying the hot summer days and the awe-inspiring views over the Bay of Gibraltar.

David had taken a moment to enjoy them too, though his view had been one quite different. His gaze followed the figure in the water, his eyes locking onto the sheer ivory white bikini as she power-stroked through the crystal blue water from one edge to the other. Without stopping, she dived under, rolled and kicked away from the wall to repeat the lap.

She did this five times before swerving and swimming towards the edge closest to the villa, where they'd left their towels.

It was a scene straight out of David's own dirty little movie. Time almost seemed to hold its breath as Cassandra pulled herself up easily out of the water, throwing back her bountiful mane of raven hair. Rivulets sparkled in the sun and cascaded down her long neck, full breasts and flat belly. Then she was up on her feet and towelling her hair, her head turning up towards the house. Finding him.

Their eyes met and David knew instinctively that she knew he had been watching her.

He'd been caught, but the idea only sent a hot shiver tingling up his spine as he dragged his eyes away. Feeling a little hot, he decided he needed to take a break.

And maybe have a little fun in the sun himself...

Chapter *Two*

"Ah… this is the life!" Stacey sighed, stretched out across her inflatable.

Cassandra didn't answer, just led back on her float and kicked gently away from the edge, sending her float drifting lazily back across the surface of the pool. Overhead, the sky was as blue as she had ever seen it. Stretched out below at the base of the western slope of the rock that dominated the eastern side, the slender crescent shaped town of Gibraltar seemed quiet and sleepy. Beyond that, the still azure waters of the bay stretched out as far as the eye could see towards the black lines of the distant Spanish coast.

It was paradise. Their very own little slice of heaven. Cut away from the rest of the world the way Gibraltar itself was separated from the rest of mainland Europe.

So then why couldn't she bring herself to enjoy it?

'I'm sorry, Cass, but you're just too boring for me,' Nathan's voice answered, ringing through her memory, thick with all the self-assured arrogance she had once found so exciting.

Now it only made her skin crawl.

It shouldn't have mattered. They'd only gone out a couple of times. Hell, they hadn't even slept together yet. Not that he hadn't been trying, of course.

It shouldn't have mattered to her what he thought. But it did.

It mattered. She hated that it did, but it did matter to her.

It mattered because she'd always been *that* girl. The plain Jane that played everything safe, with her routine and comfort zones. Unadventurous. Unspontaneous. Boring.

"Hey Cassy, are you listening?" Stacey asked, loud enough to snap Cassandra out of her daze.

"Huh? What? Oh, sorry Stace…"

Pushing her sunglasses up into her sleek and tidy blonde bob, Stacey rolled over to fix Cassandra with a look. Concern shadowed her pale blue eyes. "Are you okay?"

"What?" Cassandra forced a smile that she knew wouldn't reach her eyes. "Course I am… why… why wouldn't I be?"

"How about because you've done nothing but mope since we got here." She was right, of course. "Geez, girl, I told you the guy was bad news."

"N-no… it's just… err… Stace… do you think I'm boring?" Cassandra blurted out.

"What? No! Did he tell you that?" Stacey demanded, bolting up so fast the inflatable wobbled dangerously.

"Pretty much… he just wanted to make it clear. It was definitely me, not him."

"How *thoughtful*," Stacey sneered, then her expression softened as she reached over to touch her friend's shoulder. "Cass… you like what makes you feel comfortable, that's all. There is nothing wrong with that. It doesn't make you boring, just you. And if that fucker can't accept it, then that's on him. You are a great catch. So what if you're not that adventurous. With a bod like yours, any guy would be drooling to go out with you. You just need to show it off now and then."

"What with my fat ass and belly?" Stacey rolled her eyes. "I still can't believe you made me buy this thing. I wear more in the shower."

"What? It looks great on you. You've got all the right curves for a bikini, and your tits look great in it. All you need now is a sexy little skirt to show off your legs and maybe a…" Cassandra's stomach dropped as her friend's eyes lit up with an all too familiar look. Oh no, she wasn't thinking… "I know, why don't we go across the border and hit the town for a girl's night? Do a little shopping in Puerto Banus. Have a few drinks. Find a couple of hot Spanish boys. You know what they say, the best way to get over a bad break up is getting under a hot lay..."

"Eww... no!" Cassandra laughed in mock disgust. Why was she not surprised. Shopping, drinks and sex- Stacey's holy trinity. Though not exclusively in that order.

"Aww… Okay, what about just shopping and drinks then? Come on, Cass, it's only an hour away. We can be there and back again before it even gets late. And you got all those euros for spending money… and it's the off-season, so the sales are on. Just imagine the bargains!"

"Yeah, thanks, but I think I'll pass. My girls and I are staying right here. But you go."

Stacey slumped back on her inflatable with a sigh. "Na, it's ok, I don't want to leave you all alone with Dad."

"Don't be silly, this is your break too, you go, have some fun, your dad barely comes out of his cave any way right? It'll be just like I have my own private little getaway." Even as she said it, Cassandra couldn't help a glance back towards the house, her eyes moving towards Mr Street's office window, disappointed but not surprised to find it empty.

However, Stacey was already halfway across the pool to the ledge and didn't bother to reign in her excitement as she called back, "Kay, if you're sure!"

Then she was up and out and almost skipping across the villa's back porch, before vanishing through into the kitchen without so much as a backwards wave.

Cassandra watched her go with the smallest of smiles. God bless Stacey. She always knew just what to say.

Not.

She always had the right of it, but translation got muddled in transit, somewhere between her brain and her mouth. But her heart was in the right place.

It was her idea to come out here. No sooner had Casandra told her flatmate and old childhood friend what had happened with Nathan, she was on the phone to their boss getting them both some time off. Stacey never left anything to chance and knew Cassandra well enough to know she would likely try weaselling out of what she had planned by simply saying she couldn't get the time off. Only as an afterthought had she then called her dad to ask if they could use his villa in Gibraltar for the week, with an extra helping of the daddy's little princess routine just to make sure.

She needn't have bothered. Mr. Street had always been cool like that, even before his divorce. Firm but laid back, and a big strong softie with a softer spot just for his daughter and her friends.

Or it might have had something to do with the fact he'd already been out here and wouldn't have to worry about his nice tidy villa getting trashed by a pair of boozed up party girls.

Not that he'd have had much to worry about on her account. Stacey might have been the good-time girl, but being the boring little introvert that she was, Cassandra rarely ever went out to party. And she never, ever got pissed.

I'm sorry, Cass, but you're just too boring for me.

No! Inwardly screaming defiance, she rolled off the inflatable and plugged down through the pool's crystal waters. After the warmth of the Mediterranean sun, the depths raked her like shards of ice as she kicked angrily for the bottom, then rolled and torpedoed from the tiles for the surface, breaching up to grab a breath before breast stroking for the edge. Nathan's words constantly echoed in her ears, taunting her.

No, that wasn't who she was. Stacey was right. She'd prove that arrogant son of a bitch wrong. She could step out of her comfort zone. She could do the unexpected.

She could… She would… Oh, who the fuck was she kidding?

Hauling herself out of the frigid waters, she made straight for the lounger where she'd laid out her towel, lying back and wrapping it around her like a cocoon. It was hopeless. If she didn't even have the balls to go out on an impromptu shopping trip with her best friend, how the hell was she ever going to break out of her slump?

What could she do to break the cycle?

Who-

"Room for one more?"

Chapter *Three*

The familiar, low rasp sent a hot rush sizzling down her spine and tingling out to her fingertips.

Oh god, that voice!

Her heart suddenly fluttered like a robin red-breast in a cage and Cassandra's breath caught in her throat as she twisted round and saw *him* walking out of the house.

David Street, Stacey's dad. A god among mortal men.

A feast to behold, he was tall with long limbs, dressed in tan shorts, sandals and a plain white short-sleeved shirt that stretched tight over broad musculature. Beneath those thick waves of raven black hair, his face was like a chiselled slab of white marble, hard and brutal with a sharp nose, wide jaw rough with the morning's growth, and full lips she had so longed to feel pressed against her skin.

And his eyes were the stormiest shade of grey she had ever seen, and so intense, they seemed to crash over the banks of her own and wash her away.

"Oh, hey Mr Street." Cassandra forced herself to smile, but couldn't drag her gaze from the vision of him coming to stand over her with a colourful drink in hand. It didn't help that he'd left the top three buttons of his shirt open, teasing her with a glimpse of the treasure beneath. "Sure, help yourself."

Oh if only I could… David mused, drinking in the bounty stretched out before him, before stepping around her lounger and instead settling down on the next. "Thanks, how's the sun?" he asked before sipping his drink.

"Hot and bright. Just another beautiful day in paradise," she said, forcing a broad smile and trying to remember she was meant to be on holiday. She was supposed to be enjoying herself, not a bag of nerves just because her friend's dad was sitting next to her. Sitting next to her while she was dressed in nothing but this damn micro bikini!

Then he chuckled, a deep warbling rumble that rose up from within his throat to crash over Cassandra as he turned to look at her. "You say that now, but give it a couple more months and you'll be pinning for some good old English weather."

She could feel his eyes moving over her body, devouring her from head to toe, and the heat of his gaze made her skin flush and tingle.

"If you say so…." She licked her lips nervously, her mouth suddenly dry. "How's your book coming along?"

Realising he was staring, David quickly dragged his eyes back out across the bay. Past the menagerie of brightly coloured sail ships, an immense cargo tanker was cutting through the dark turquoise waters towards the Spanish port. He focused on it, trying to ignore the stirring between his legs. It didn't help.

"Oh… you know, it's coming along, about as well as British Rail. I've got the nucleus of a plot, but it's missing… something. I don't know. It's there, right in front of me, but I just can't see through the block."

"The dreaded block huh, is there anything I can do?"

Oh, he could think of a few ways.

Every author had their ways of dealing with writer's block. It was just an unpleasant fact of life in his trade, like taxes, the government, or Amazon's ever shifting policies. Making a big deal about them wasn't going to make any difference, you just had to be practical and deal with it. Sex had always been a great help for him when trying to get over the wall.

Fuck, how long had it been since he'd last gotten laid? Three months? Four, at least. Not since his divorce. Too long. Much too long if just looking at Cassandra in that sexy little thing was getting him hard.

He'd need to do something about that once the girls had gone home.

But first, he needed to make it through the next few days without making a fool of himself.

He coughed, trying to drag his attention back to the tanker, the coast, a bird, anything but the flawless curves of the beauty beside him! Dammit, just being so close to her was a fucking turn on. "No, not unless you can slow down time, get the publisher's off my back or know a trick for breaking down the wall."

She hummed for a moment, as if actually mulling it over. "Afraid I'm fresh out of ideas, though I might know a guy with an undead dragon that could deal with that wall of yours."

"Thanks, but I already have an ex-wife," he joked, and they both chuckled. It was official. Ex-wife jokes were funny no matter the situation. "So, where's my daughter scampered off to?"

"Shopping, where else?" Willing herself not to look at him, Cassandra forced a chuckle, the same one she used whenever customers told the same bad joke she'd heard a hundred times before. "The sales are on in Puerto Banus and she's been dying for a chance to splurge."

She could do this. It was just Mr Street.

The man she had known almost as long as she could remember.

Who had indulged her girlish princess fantasies when she was eight and had jokingly promised to marry her when she was all grown up.

That used to take her and Stacey to dance class every Saturday.

Her best friend's recently divorced and sexy as hell dad, who she'd spent years fantasising about.

David couldn't help another chuckle of his own. His daughter was nothing if not consistent. "Ah yes, as you said, where else." He took another sip of his cocktail, a crystal drop of condensation rolling down the glass to touch his lips as the sun beat down on them, the air growing hotter by the moment. Or maybe it was the alcohol.

Considering the already almost half empty glass before deciding he'd had enough for now, he laid it down gently in a shady spot before rounding on her. "So she just left you here all alone?"

The concern in his tone was so disarming, Casandra met his gaze without thinking and touched his shoulder with a placating hand. The contact sent a thrill racing through her fingertips. "It's okay, I don't really feel like hitting the town now and anyway, I'm not alone. You're here with me." The words were out before she could stop them, and the confession made her cheeks burn. Yet she didn't look away.

Yes, she was all alone with her bestie's daddy at his Gibraltar Villa.

Out in the wilds, miles from anywhere or anyone who could hear her scream- or beg as his sexy mouth did such wicked things between her... Dammit!

Why did he always make her feel this way?

Then Stacey's words echoed in her ears. The best way to get over a man is under one...

"You poor girl," David cooed playfully. "Trapped on the Rock with just this decrepit old man for company."

She couldn't resist the bait. "Aww... you're not so old, and the silver fox look is a classic for a reason."

"Cheeky minx!" he snapped in mock outrage, but couldn't keep the corner of his mouth from curling. "You're not too old to go over my knee, you know, young lady."

She shrieked girlishly, playing along in her best upper-class voice and squealed, "Oh no, don't spank me, please, Mr Street!"

The mock innocence of the words sent a thrill racing down to the base of David's spine, igniting thoughts of her bending over to bear the swells of her luscious derriere for his judgement, trembling slightly as she awaited the sting of his hand striking her flawless skin.

Just the thought of it stirred his desire to a rod of iron.

"No, really," he forced out, crossing his legs, inwardly cursing and trying in vain to coax the beast back into its cage. "What are you doing here with me? Why didn't what's-his-name come along, ugh… you know, that guy with the funny hair…"

"Nathan."

Just saying his name brought the taste of ash to her mouth. No, she didn't want to think about him, not here, not with Mr Street, when she'd just been starting to forget him. But the dam had cracked, and no sooner had the words left her lips, her eyes had burned with hot, salty tears as all her buried emotions suddenly boiled to the surface. "He dumped me."

"Oh God, Cass, I'm… I'm so sorry." David didn't know what else to say. What else was there to say?

He'd never met the boy, but Stacey had told him about Cassandra's new boyfriend once or twice and there had been a few pictures of the two together on Facebook.

He had rather reminded him of Justin Bieber.

He just had one of those faces he couldn't help wanting to slap.

Somehow, however, he got the feeling voicing that thought wouldn't help very much.

He'd never really been a great one for dealing with emotions. It was one reason his ex-wife had listed as grounds for divorce. Siting him as a cold, unreachable iceberg of a man who had sucked all the joy and happiness from her life. She had even gone so far as to use it to justify her rampant extramarital nymphomania, saying it was just a way of seeking the warmth of human comfort. The honourable judge Blackwood had been sympathetic but expressed the suggestion that if that were the case, he would have thought one lover would have been enough, rather than five. For his part, David had just said he was one of the old school and as such, an ardent follower of the philosophy *actions speak louder than words*.

With the dedication and spirit of all true believers, heedless of his body's treacherous desire, he wrapped an arm around her and drew her close.

She was shaking as all the unsaid hurt and emotion that had welled up inside her suddenly burst its banks. "He said I was dull and boring and passionless and couldn't-" Her words dissolved into thick wet sobs as the tears came and she just buried her face into the crook of his neck.

David couldn't bear it.

"Then he's a fool," he promised, crushing her to him. "You're a wonderful person, Cass. You deserve better than that and you should be with someone who knows how special you are, who knows how lucky he is to have you."

She didn't respond, just kept sobbing, so he held her close and waited for the storm to pass. Yet his *little brain* couldn't help but notice how well she fit in his arms, the sun-warmed softness of her skin, and the way the heavy weight of her full breasts were squashed against his chest.

No, dammit, don't think like that, you dirty old sod!

He chided himself, but when he took a breath to clear his brain, he only inhaled the sweet fragrance of her hair, still with hints of her wild berry scented shampoo.

Then it was suddenly over. She was still, her breathing deep and even as she looked up at him from beneath her dark bangs, the last wet tear sparkling down her cheeks in the sunlight. "Thanks, Mr Street… er, Stacey told me the same thing."

"Well, she's rarely wrong." He forced a reassuring grin.

She blushed and looked away, out towards the coast, unable to meet his eyes, while resisting the urge to snuggle closer. Cassandra revelled in their closeness, the feel of his arms enveloping her, holding her close and tight.

She never wanted the moment to end. "I'm sorry… I don't know what came over me." She made to pull away…

Except David wouldn't let her go. "It's okay, we all need to let go sometimes," he soothed gently, cupping her chin and gently turning her to face him, before gently brushing the tear away with his thumb. "Break-ups can be tough."

They were so close, Cassandra felt like she was getting drunk on him. His scent, his warmth, his very presence was enveloping her, intoxicating her. All it would take was one little push onto tiptoes, and she would finally know if those lips tasted as good as she'd imagined.

"Was that how it was for you? With your divorce?" The words were out before she could stop them, and when his hand dropped away, she would have done anything to take them back. "I'm sorry, I shouldn't have… forget I said anything. It's none of my business."

Again he held her fast, refusing to let her pull away, denying her any chance of escape.

"No, no, it's fine," he urged, sighing and running a hand through his hair. "My marriage was over years ago. It just took me a while to figure it out. Then I just didn't want it to, so I threw myself into my work to avoid it, but it was only a matter of time. After that, well, I just didn't really care anymore."

She couldn't help herself. There was an edge to his voice she'd never heard before. It sounded darkly dangerous, and very sexy. "So it doesn't bother you at all?"

"It did, at first," he growled. "When I found out, but not because of what she'd done. Only that she'd done it behind my back, rather than just come out and tell me she wanted a divorce."

"Did she say anything after?"

"No, what was there to say?" he said simply, before reaching down for his cocktail and bringing it up to his mouth. Cassandra's mouth dried as he swallowed the colourful contents of the glass, his head arching back and the muscles of his neck rising and falling while the first drops of perspiration rolled down his skin.

Cassandra's nails bit into her palms. They were close enough for her to lean in and lick up the drops.

"Do you blame yourself for… what happened?"

"No." He shrugged, then laughed. He actually laughed, a deep rich sound that rolled over her like dark chocolate. "We just married too young, settled down too soon, then grew apart. Becky wanted one thing, and I wanted another."

Their eyes met, and the contact sent a fresh wave of heat and awareness ebbing through her. Instinctively, she looked away. "So… what are you drinking? "

"This?" He raised the near empty glass, almost as if he was toasting her. "It's a Tequila Sunset."

Cassandra arched a brow. "Isn't it a bit early?"

"I won't tell if you don't," David shrugged, his eyes bright with mischief. "And hey, when in Spain…"

"But isn't Tequila Mexican?"

"Smart ass," he grinned ruefully. "Actually, the indigenous Mexican Indians brewed a fermented liquor from the same plant. What we know as Tequila was concocted by the Conquistadors after their brandy ran out, making Tequila actually Spanish and Spain's only indisputable, worthwhile contribution to western civilisation. Just the thing for out here in the tropics. All the kick, but none of the mess."

He raised the glass to finish it, but at the sight of the drink swirling within the glass, Cassandra couldn't resist. "Could I try? Just a sip."

"My dear girl, there's nothing but a sip left."

"Please Mr Street, I left my water in the kitchen and it's so warm out here…" she asked sweetly, batting her eyelashes.

Tempting minx

David cursed inwardly, his cock twitching at her little act. Dammit, the thing would start hurting if he didn't get out of here. Forcing his smile to stay in place, he shifted ever so slightly to pass her the glass. "Help yourself."

And that was when she saw it.

It was only a momentary glance as she reached to take the offered drink, but it was enough. Enough for her to note the bulge straining against his thigh through the fabric of his shorts, thick and huge. Enough to send a shiver racing through her and to have her grabbing the offered cocktail, downing it in one go.

God, had she done that to him?

Then their eyes met again, over the rim of the empty glass, and the warmth of the spirit raced down to burn between her legs. It made her brave, ready to take a leap.

Still holding his gaze, she lowered the glass back to the ground, before slowly sliding her tongue across her lips, collecting the last of the fruit-laced bravery there. Then, moaning a throaty purr, she asked, "Mr Street, would you mind putting some sunscreen on my back for me?

Chapter *Four*

David's blood ran cold at the question.

"I don't know if that's such a good idea, Cass. "

Yes, that was it. Cass was the name he always used when he was playing the role of the adult. That was what he needed now, to be an adult, to set boundaries. To get the hell out of here and back to his office before he did something really stupid.

However, Cassandra glimpsed his other head twitching against its prison.

"Aww, how come?" she cooed, all innocence and sweetness, scooping up and offering him her bottle of factor 40, silently praying her nerve held. "Please, Mr Street. You don't want me to get burned now, do you?"

David stared at the bottle like it was a coiled viper, poised to strike. This was his last chance. He needed to go.

Just get up and go back inside. He could do it. Just get up and go. He had to, before…

Taking it from her, he rose up and walked around her lounger to stand over her before popping the cap. "Roll over."

The command was clipped and said with such primal authority, it sent a fresh shiver of excitement tingling through Cassandra. She obeyed immediately. Rolling onto her front, she pulled the wash of her raven hair aside before starting on the fastenings of her top.

"I think that's going too far."

"But I'll have tan lines, Mr Street," she implored, barely able to keep still for the thought of his hands on her bare skin. Just managing to finger the knot loose despite the knots in her tummy, she added sweetly, "I know you'll be a gentleman and not look."

"Of course not," he bit out, squeezing a generous amount of the sunscreen onto his palm before smearing a long line across her shoulder blades. It wasn't cold. Not after a morning sitting out under the Mediterranean sun, but she shivered and squirmed all the same as his hand circled around and around, teasing down her long neck and across her shoulders, massaging it in.

He worked until he had applied it all and then kept going. Her skin was just so warm, so butter soft. He couldn't get enough.

And nor could Cassandra.

"Mmm… that feels so nice Mr Street… mmm… lower," she panted, burying her face in the lounger to keep him from spying the blush heating her face. God, what was she doing? This was Mr Street, her best friend's dad.

This was insane, but she didn't care.

She'd been dreaming of this moment. This intimacy with him.

Cassandra had craved the feeling of his hands sliding over her skin, the sensations those big, powerful hands would send sizzling straight down to her throbbing centre.

If this was her one moment with him, then she intended to make it count and enjoy every second.

David was happy to indulge her and applied a fresh squeeze of lotion.

Guided by her soft, kittenish moans, he worked his way down the delicate curve of her back, his thumb playing along her spine like the strings of a violin while his fingers danced along her ribs. Accidentally, one finger brushed along the side of her milky white breast and she sucked in a breath that made his cock tighten and twitch.

Fuck, this was bad. He needed to get out of here, away, back to the safety of his office. A place he could look but not touch. Never touch! This was Cassandra, for Christ's sake. His daughter's best friend. Her fucking flatmate!

Needing to put some much-needed distance between them, he manoeuvred to the base of the lounger, dragging his hands around the contours of her upturned derriere and down her gloriously long legs. He tried to focus, to clear his thoughts, but the distance only made it easier for him to devour the vision of her stretched out before him. His eyes immediately locked onto the small triangle of white material between her legs. Still slightly damp from her earlier swim, her folds were clearly visible against the fabric, the nub of her clit swollen and pleading for attention, betraying her arousal.

This was affecting her just as much as it was him.

And that revelation made it impossible for him to pull away.

He worked his way back up from her ankle and along her calf. Stroking and brushing, his touch as light and teasing as a feather, the premise of applying the lotion forgotten, making her writhe and moan. Then, as his fingers brushed over her inner thighs, she raised her hips and subtly parted her legs just that bit wider, opening herself to him.

It was all the permission he needed.

Cassandra couldn't stand it. His hands were working her into a frenzy, making her skin tingle wherever he touched. She had to grab the edges of the lounger to battle against the urge to slip a hand beneath her suit and soothe the fire throbbing between her legs.

Was this really happening?

Was she really letting him do this?

Him! Mr Street, her best friend's daddy, was touching her! No, not just touching her, massaging her, seducing her with his every touch. How long had she dreamed of this moment, of his hands on her skin, sliding up her legs, finger tips pressing higher and higher and-

She bit down on a surprised squeak as something brushed across her folds.

David slowly brushed his thumb along her folds, tracing them through the swimsuit, feeling the heat and wetness burning there. Somewhere deep, deep down, the moral man he'd been was desperately trying to drag his

hand away. Screaming that this was wrong, that they needed to stop, but he couldn't resist. All her sexy little moans were driving him crazy.

Cassandra didn't object, nor did she move at all. She lay still beneath him, trembling as goose flesh rose across her legs, her breath coming hot and ragged as he stoked the liquid heat throbbing in her core.

This wasn't the sweet and innocent girl he'd known and watched playing with dolls, pretending to be a Disney princess. That child was gone. She was a woman now. A lush and beautiful creature, with all a woman's primitive hungers and needs.

She needed him.

And he was happy to oblige, gently pressing down, rubbing the pad of his thumb around her, feeling the heat burn. His fingers traced along the line of her thong, teasing around the fabric. His fingers caressed along her inner thighs before pushing beneath her suit into lush heat, making her gasp and roll her hips against him, inclining back and opening herself completely to his invading digits.

He leaned down and whispered in her ear. "This is a *very* bad idea."

"No!" she sobbed in protest, squeezing her eyes shut against the rush of tingling pleasure as his finger curled to stroke the spot. "Please, I've wanted this for so long, Mr Street- oh!" Her breath caught when his thumb strummed her covered clit, making her writhe beneath him. "I-I-I won't tell anyone… please, I'll be… such a good girl for you… I'll never tell a soul… please…"

"Good, because even if I wanted to, I can't stop now," he promised, withdrawing the finger from her heat and offering it to her, teasing the pad across her soft pink lips. Obediently Cassandra opened and her pink tongue flicked out, tentatively tasting the cream coating the digit. She drew him in and her cheeks hollowed as she sucked it clean.

It was such an erotic display. If he were a younger man, he might have succumbed to his lust right there.

Age had its compensations.

Instead, he dipped his head and laid a feather soft kiss on her nape. It was a surprisingly intimate gesture given their current position, and she gasped a soft breathy moan as he did it again, and again, trailing kisses down her back. Slowly. So slowly. Slow enough to make her wriggle beneath him as the heated tension inside her wound in ever tighter knots with each flutter of his tongue. And as he kissed down the soft curve of her lower back, his fingers hooked under the strings of her bikini bottoms and dragged them down her legs.

The heady perfume of her desire greeted him, invading his senses, making his mouth water. With his cock straining against its bonds, growing evermore uncomfortable by the second, he pulled back to admire his handiwork. "You're so beautiful."

It was the first time anyone had ever said that to her. Cassandra felt her skin burn with a heat that had nothing to do with the desire throbbing inside her. "No, please don't stare at me like that..."

"But I want to," he growled, raising one hand to caress her derriere, marvelling at the silky softness of her skin. God, she was just so perfect. Her ex must have been mad to even consider breaking up with her.

Shifting his hands ever so slightly, cupping the perfect handfuls of her cheeks, he spread them just enough to reveal the crinkled flesh of her rosebud and the slick, swollen folds below. "Mmm… you're so wet, you naughty girl."

"Oh god, no please, this is so embarrassing, I can't help-oh!" Her voice left her in a gasp when the tip of his tongue swirled around her pucker, sweeping and flitting and driving her wild. "No… please… not there… that's so… dirty…"

"Yeah, and you like it, don't you?" He switched tact, his hands drawing her to him while tonguing her tight little rosebud.

"Yes!" she sobbed, her back arching even as the world melted down to just the illicit feeling of his slick tongue driving through her sphincter to feast on her little asshole.

God, she couldn't believe she was letting him do this. And she couldn't believe how good it felt. Though no virgin, Cassandra had never let any past lover play with her butt. She'd just never been able to see how anyone could draw pleasure from doing such things, but with Mr Street, it all just clicked. There was nothing she wouldn't do for him, and her body knew it, relished it.

Her body demanded it.

"Yeah, good girl…" he purred against her pucker, smirking inwardly as it made her shiver, working his tongue in and out against the clutch of her hole. "What do you want?"

"W-what? Oh… oh god… please… I-I-wait!" Panic flaring at the feeling of his tongue leaving her, she threw a look back over her shoulder to see him smirking back at her. "Don't… don't stop… please…"

With eyes dark and gleaming with a savage hunger, he seductively licked the taste of her from his lips. "Mmm… you've got such a tasty ass Cassandra, I could eat it for days…"

"No, don't say that…" She'd never heard Mr Street talk like that before. She liked it. His crude words sent sensations tingling through her, hardening her nipples to tight points that ached to be sucked, before he rushed downwards once more.

"Then tell me what you want," he purred, bending down to touch his lips to her hole in a soft butterfly kiss. Then, slowly kneading the lush curves of her derriere, spreading them wide, he gave the flesh between a long languorous lick. "Go on, you dirty girl, give yourself over to your desires. Tell me the things you think about while playing with your pretty pink pussy. What naughty fantasies bring you to that hot, sticky end…"

"I can't… please… it's embarrassing." She couldn't keep from panting now. Her heart pounded harder as he repeated the slow lick again and again. Each one a little longer than the last and she couldn't resist wriggling her hips back at him as the tip of his wicked tongue neared the font of her heat throbbing between her legs. A deliciously naughty jolt zipped straight through her centre.

She didn't know how much longer she'd last if he kept this up. Why did it have to feel so good?

And then…

"If you say so…" The husky rasp of his voice tingled against her inner thighs, making her shudder and whimper. Then he dragged his tongue down her sex, through her swollen folds to flutter over her clit. Sweeping and swirling, stirring her lower belly into a wet, throbbing blaze.

Cassandra couldn't stand it.

"Oh… oh god… no… please… don't make me say it… I… I…" Back bowing, she squeezed her eyes shut against the storm, but it wasn't enough. She was shaking, her climax building.

"Tell me, Cassandra."

That voice. The way it commanded her name, ordering her to obey. She was powerless to resist as he thrust his tongue deep inside her creamy centre, pushing her over the edge and licking her through her release. Each sweep of his tongue prolonged the waves crashing over her, pushing her higher and higher, until the words flew from her in a gasp… "Fuck me, Mr Street!"

Chapter *Five*

"Good girl," David praised, savouring this view of her, bent over, quaking, mouth open yet eyes squeezed tightly shut against the orgasm that still surged through her. It was such a surreal image. This innocent girl he'd watch grow up dissolved into a wanton little sex kitten, beautiful and innocent yet primitive, desperate, and so fucking sexy.

He wanted to ingrain it into his memory forever and guided one of her legs up and over as he did, rolling her onto her back.

Cassandra went willingly, panting, basking in the sweet afterglow. Her eyes opened, searching, pleading. "Please… Mr Street… fuck me, please…"

"Shhh… Cass," he'd reverted to that familiar easy tone she knew so well, and said the words so softly, for a moment, she dared hope this sweet torture was about to end, and all her fantasises were about to come true.

"I love watching you cum." He swooped down, tasting her with a long lick along her sex.

"Oh god!" Cassandra gasped, her back arching at the toe-curling contact.

She couldn't stand it. He was driving her insane. She wanted to twist and writhe away from that oh so sinfully wicked mouth. To grab her tits, pinch her nipples, finger her clit. To bury her hands in his hair and force his mouth just where she needed it.

Yet she couldn't. Her ecstatic body wasn't listening to her anymore.

"Mmm… Yeah, you like that, Cass? Want more?" he purred, dragging the flat of his tongue back up through her folds to circle her little nub. "You've got the sweetest little pussy, so warm and slick. I can't wait to feel you wrapped around my cock, squeezing me like a tight little fist as I make you cum. Do you want me to make you cum? Would you like that? Want me to make you feel good and this tight little pussy purr?" He dipped his head to cover her clit with his mouth, his checks hollowing as he sucked, igniting sparks behind her eyes.

It was too much. Struck by the sheer eroticism of seeing the man's head between her legs, feeling him devouring her with his wicked, sinfully dirty mouth, she was like a ship caught in a tempest. Her fingers clutched the lounger's cushion in a deathly grip.

"Yes! Please, Mr street… oh fuck… oh my god… oh yes… yes, eat my pussy, it's all yours… oh fuck. I'm cumming, I'm cumming!"

He growled, loving this side of her. It was a side of her he had never known. Should have never known. A side of her that was as forbidden to him as the infamous fruit was to Adam. And like all forbidden fruit, she was all the sweeter for it. He loved this view of her luscious body arching from between her smooth thighs, the sight of her flushed with passion, wild with desire, the sounds of her pleasure, the feeling of her shuddering around him.

Yet it couldn't slake his thirst for her, his hunger for more. He wanted more. He wanted all of her, completely and absolutely, to spoil her for any other man, to make her his. "Fuck, you cum so easily. Yeah, do it again, Cass, cum for me."

"Yes! Yes! Oh god, oh Jesus… that feels so good… Mr… Mr street, you're- oh fuck!"

"Yeah, what do you want, Cass?" he pressed, as he lapped at her making sure she could feel every syllable beat through her tasty little sex as his greedy tongue pushed through her spasming tissues to drink from the very centre of her erogenous being.

His cock tightened dangerously, desperate for attention and jealous of his tongue.

It was all he could do not to go balls deep in her luscious pussy right then and there.

"Fuck me," she moaned, squirming and writhing as her body dissolved. God, Nathan had never done this to her, never made her feel this way. It was like his tongue had a mind of its own and knew just where to touch her, what to do to drive her wild. It was too much, too good…

"Louder." There was a delicious, almost devilish edge to his words now, and she knew he was enjoying toying with her.

"Fuck me!" The words left her in a shriek, her head rolling as he worked her into a storm, her body shaking with the tension of her building release as she suddenly tittered on the brink. "I want you to fuck me, Mr Street! Use me any way you want. That's your pussy. Bury your big dick in me. Make me your whore. I'll be a good little fuck toy for you. I'll… I'll… oh god… oh fuck I'm gonna cum… I'm gonna- oh god, don't stop, don't… stop… oh… god…" Then her release exploded through the hot, throbbing knot at her core, the waves surging over her, sending her reeling, soaring like no orgasm that had come before it, shaking her to her foundations, leaving her basking in a sea of stars.

Only when she had finally stopped shaking did David abandon his newfound treasure, but not before attending to her fully bared jewel with a soft, almost chaste kiss. She arched and gasped excitedly, her clit still too tender and sensitive from such a powerful climax for any more direct stimulation just yet.

And the knowledge that it was he who had brought this little sultry vixen so much pleasure and had pushed her over the shattering brink with just his mouth, filled him with such a primitive pride, he just couldn't help himself.

Coming back down to earth, blinking through the black spots dancing before her eyes, Cassandra was treated to the view of David standing before her with his trousers open, fisting his imperious cock.

It was a scene straight out of her dirtiest dreams. Yet they were only fantasies. Pale shadows of the reality of the Adonis standing before her. Over her. Almost close enough for her to taste his salty musk. All she would have to do was lean up and open her mouth…

"See something you like, baby?" he purred, watching her with dark, hungry eyes. He watched her as he stroked the full length of his cock with slow pumps that made the thick crest swell and glisten beneath the warm Mediterranean sun.

It was the most erotic thing she'd ever seen and made her still tingling pussy throb needily.

Her mouth suddenly dry, she could only nod. Her eyes reverted to the view of his thick cock, which now seemed so much bigger than she'd expected.

A hell of a lot bigger than Nathan's, that was for sure.

Her heart racing, she slowly raised her legs, bracing the flat of her feet on the sunbed, baring herself to those hungry eyes, inviting him to finish what he'd started.

He accepted immediately, covering her body with his and crushing his mouth to hers, kissing her hungrily. His wicked tongue slipped between her lips to tangle with hers, the very same tongue that just moments before had been devouring her.

She moaned at such a dirty thought and greedily sucked his tongue, her hips arching up, curling against the weight of his desire, desperate to get it where she wanted it. Where she needed him. The head of his cock, hot and slick with pre-cum, slipped and slid between their bodies and left a slick trail down her belly to…

David pulled away, dragging his mouth from hers with a low growl.

"You're so beautiful, Cass…" he growled, breathless, his voice hot and hungry, eyes holding hers as his crown pressed against her slick folds. "If you want to stop-"

Shaking her head, Cassandra didn't give him a chance to finish. Stop? Like hell, she'd been waiting all her life to have him like this. No way was she about to stop now. Wrapping her legs around his waist and arching her hips, she urged him on, digging her heels into his backside so…

"Oh… fuck!" she gasped, her heart thundering in her ears as the world shrank down to the feeling of *him* inside her, his broad crest pressing through her sex, stretching her to her limit, filling her inch by delicious inch.

Oh god, it was too much! He was too much, too thick, too hard, too… big!

No, not big, huge, hung like a fucking stallion!

David could only groan a low, choked sound at the feeling of sliding into her warmth, her plush heat wrapping around him, sucking him in. It was the sweetest torture. Just watching her sexy little mouth open with that first sweet shock of penetration, her eyes widening, losing focus, rolling back before snapping forward in the rush of wild, untamed pleasure.

Fuck, it was a miracle he hadn't cum already.

He knew he needed to be patient, to wait and let her adjust, but the urge, the need to take her, to rut, to fuck, to claim this little sex kitten as his own, was inexorable.

"M-Mr Street… Please…" Cassandra wasn't entirely sure what she was pleading for.

The words left her in a rush as he rolled his hips, pulling out a little before driving back in.

Her back bowed up and off the sunbed at the feeling of being stretched so deliciously and stuffed to her limits. And not just in the physical sense. This feeling, the connection between them, the way he was watching her, it was all so intense. Way too intense. She'd never felt anything like it. Desperate to burn the feeling of him inside her to memory, she clenched around him.

"Oh fuck," David hissed, squeezing his eyes shut against the sudden rush that nearly pushed him over the edge. "Don't do that…"

"Mmm… sorry," she panted, provocatively biting her lip. She wasn't sorry, god she loved the way his cock was twitching inside her, thickening and hardening all the more.

"Oh, you naughty girl, so that's the way you want to play it, huh?"

It happened so fast she could barely react, her pleasure drunk brain only really registering the way his cock surged inside her as the flair of his hips spread her thighs wide, opening her up in the very best of ways while those powerful hands raised her legs, guiding them up over his shoulders.

"Is this what you want?" he asked, staring down at her, gently, rocking his hips to emphasise his meaning as his hands ran down her legs to seize her waist. His hold was gentle, but firm, powerful, unescapable, and kept her pinned against his abdomen at just the right angle for her to see where their bodies joined.

"Yes…" she gasped, trying to meet his teasing roll with one of her own, but was restrained by the hold he had on her.

"Does it feel good?"

"Yes…" She could feel tears welling up in the corners of her eyes as each time he circled his hips, the flat of his abdomen ground over her clit. Growing desperate, maddened by the subtle tease of friction, she twisted and writhed, needing to break free, her hands tearing at the lounger's cushion for any sort of leverage.

"You want more?"

"Oh… god… please, Mr… Street… you're… I… I'm…" Oh god, why was he being so cruel? She was so hot, hotter for it than she had ever been. Couldn't he see that? See how badly she wanted him?

"That's it, Cas, let it go, tell me what you want…" His voice was soft and low, but the predatory gleam in his eyes was pure deviance. He pulled back until just the tip remained inside her, leaving her feeling cold and empty.

Yet the sight of his cock, rising from her depths, wet and shiny with her cream, was unquestionably the sexiest thing she had ever seen.

"Yes, I want more! More! Fuck me more! Bury that big dick in me. Pound my tight little pussy, that's your pussy, give it to me… give it to me- oh my god, oh my god, oh my go-oh!" Her pleas dissolved in a long moan as he drove back into her, going balls deep within her slick, eager walls in one smooth drive.

"That's right, Cas, you're mine now, mine. These beautiful tits. This tight little cunt. All mine." He punctuated each claim with another curl of his hips, withdrawing and thrusting, emphasising his claims, determined to make sure she would never forget.

And she quickly lost herself in the feeling of his thick cock stretching her, filling her like nothing she had ever imagined.

"Yes. Yes! Yours, all yours! Oh god, hold me down, make me take it, make me watch your big fucking cock pound my little pussy, oh fuck, feels so good," Cassandra moaned, her head rolling and her back bowing up off the lounger, offering her body up to him, letting him use her as he wanted, however he wanted.

And David couldn't get enough of her.

Sex had never been like this with his ex. To her, for all her extramarital activities, the Kama Sutra was a menu in an Indian takeaway. She'd been greedy and demanding, selfish in the quest for her own release.

Cassandra was as different as different could be and he wanted to show her how special she was, make her feel as treasured as she deserved.

Already close, he knew he couldn't last long, so rather than holding back, he gave her everything. Draw and thrust, draw and thrust, over and over again as he pounded her slick folds, going deeper with every stroke, making sure she could feel every inch of him. The wet slap of their body's meeting rang out with the squeaks and groans of the lounger beneath them.

Cassandra only moaned her approval, letting him take her, letting him take what he wanted as she moved with him, her ardour burning just as fiercely. Rocking beneath him, her tight sex clenching, squeezing him as he drove into her hard and fast, dominating her completely and sending her spiralling towards another climax.

God, if he kept this up much longer, she had no doubt she would be deliciously sore by the morning, and walking funny for days.

God, "Oh god… oh god… oh-oh M-Mr Street… Yeah… yeah… yeah… oh my god… oh- fuck! Fuck, that's so fucking good!" She couldn't stand it. It felt like the place where they were connected was melting away in a sparkling electric storm that tingled out to every nerve in her body. "Oh, fuck… oh… oh… oh my god, oh fuck, don't stop, give me that dick, use my little pussy, give me all your fucking cock, I want it, I wa- oh- Oh fuck, I'm cumming, I'm cumming all over your cock…"

She was being too loud. They were out in the open, their modesty shielded only by the small wall that encircled the property. Anyone walking by would hear them. However, Cassandra didn't give a damn. The almost nirvana-like high she was cresting left little care in her. Nothing could pull her from the incredible sensations sweeping through her like wildfire, shoving her to the point of madness.

"That's it, Cass, cum for me, cum all over my dick as I fuck your brains out!" he growled, his jaw clenched tight, fighting to hold back his inevitable climax. His taut muscles flexed deliciously beneath his skin as he loomed over her, stretching out, his hands moving up from her waist to cage her beneath him as he drove into her, fucking her through her orgasm. Sweat glistened like oil across his brow and chest. His impossibly hard cock seemed to swell inside her.

And knowing that she could do this to him, push him to the brink of his sanity, drove Cassandra wild.

"Oh my god, please, feels too good, use me however you want, that's your pussy, I just want to be your little fuck toy, I just… I just, oh god, I can't take it, it's too good. It's too good!" Her voice died away as, trembling, shaking, she was hurled from her peak to tumble through time and space, lost in the stormy throes of the orgasm of her life.

"Yes, that's it, cum, cum… cum- oh fuck!" he gasped, squeezing his eyes shut and throwing his head back in a great bare-toothed growl as her sex bore down, wrapping around and milking his cock to the point he couldn't hold back any longer. However, before he could pull out, her legs crossed, wrapping around him and locking at the ankles, drawing him in, needing to be closer.

"No… don't… leave it in… I want to feel you cum inside me Mr Street, give it to me, fill me up with all your cum!" Then her hands were in his hair and their lips crashed together as he unleased rope after rope of creamy heat deep inside her.

They clung together until the tremors passed before disentangling from each other's embrace enough to roll, so Cassandra lay astride him on the sunbed with David still inside her. Panting hard with aftershocks still zinging through her, she buried her face in the crock of his shoulder, inhaling deeply, savouring the cocktail of their mixed scents upon an air of salt and sex. Cassandra relished the feel of his powerful arms enveloping her, holding her close, his cock softening and the warmth of his seed throbbing inside her. It just felt so right, so perfect, that she wanted nothing so much as to stay like this forever.

Despite herself, she couldn't help a small chuckle.

Looking down, David arched a brow. "Something funny?"

"No, I was just thinking," she mused, trailing one hand through the curls of his dark dusting of chest hair. "When Stacey told me the best way to get over Nathan was a quick hookup, I don't think this is quite what she had in mind."

"No, I bet not." He gave a bark of laughter. "But I think I prefer our way."

"Hmm…" she agreed. Spotting a stray drop of perspiration rolling down his neck, she quickly swept it up with a sweep of her tongue, following it up all the way to his ear. "But you know what?"

"What?" His mouth twisted in that devastating smirk. Deep inside her, his still semi-hard cock reawakened, stiffening, and lengthening like a serpentine phoenix rising from the ashes.

She pulled back to meet his eyes, biting her lip. "I'm not entirely sure I'm over him just yet. Maybe I need to take another plunge under my besties' sexy daddy. What do you think?"

Thinking back to his office and his unfinished manuscript and the looming deadline, David couldn't help but grin back. "Always do what the doctor orders…" Then he kissed her and pulled her back down onto the lounger.

He had till the end of the week to finish the book.

Plenty of time.

The *End*

A Tropical Cocktail Boxset
Romance is in the air in this two book Holiday Romance
boxset that is all about sun, sea and sex…
Tequila Sunset
Beneath The Sheets

Alpha Men of the Otherworld
The battle of the Species is about to rage, and only the
true alpha will come out on top in the Lord of Lust
hottest new duo boxset that sees vampires and
werewolves lock tooth and claw…

Temptation at its Sweetest…
Book 1: The Babysitter
Book 2: The Boss's Daughter

Sweet Temptations: books 1&2 are sizzling tales that break all the rules and combine lust, seduction and temptation. Loaded with drama and heat, this boxset will ignite your ereader and leave you panting for more.

When Mina returns for her stepbrother's 21st birthday, she thinks her days of lusting after him are over. Caught up in the heat and passion of the moment, she is stunned to find them back in bed together; their feelings clearly far from resolved. Haunted by her desire, Mina now has another problem… she must head down a path of lust and desire; torn between the dark delights of the handsome bad boy down the street and her adorable stepbrother who has always been there for her. Can she confront the truth she has long tried to bury? How far will she go to save the one she wants, but knows she can never truly have?